The Lottie Project

Jacqueline Wilson

Illustrated by Nick Sharratt

CORGI YEARLING BOOKS

For Rupa Patel
(author of The Jacqueline Wilson Quiz Book)
and special thanks to everyone at
Burscough County Primary School

THE LOTTIE PROJECT
A CORGI YEARLING BOOK : 9780440863663

First published in Great Britain by Doubleday,
a division of Random House Children's Books

PRINTING HISTORY
Doubleday edition published 1997
Corgi Yearling edition published 1998

Corgi Yearling Books are published by Random House Children's Books,
61–63 Uxbridge Road, Ealing, London W5 5SA,
a division of The Random House Group Ltd.

Addresses for Random House Group Ltd companies outside the UK
can be found at: www.randomhouse.co.uk
The Random House Group Ltd Reg. No. 954009.

Made and printed in Great Britain by Cox & Wyman, Reading, Berkshire

The Random House Group Limited makes every effort to ensure that the
papers used in its books are made from trees that have been legally
sourced from well-managed and credibly certified forests. Our paper
procurement policy can be found at: www.randomhouse.co.uk/paper.htm.

SCHOOL

I knew exactly who I was going to sit next to in class. Easy-peasy, simple-pimple. It was going to be Angela, with Lisa sitting at the nearest table to us. I'm never quite sure if I like Lisa or Angela best, so it's only fair to take turns.

Jo said what if Angela and Lisa want to sit together with *you* behind or in front or at the side. I just smiled at her. I don't want to sound disgustingly boastful but I'm the one Angela and Lisa are desperate to sit next to. Lots of the girls want to be best friends with me, actually. I'm just best friends with Lisa and Angela, but anyone can be in our special Girls' Gang. Any girl. No boys allowed. That goes without saying. Even though I just did.

But guess what happened that first day of term. We got this new teacher. We knew we wouldn't be getting Mrs Thomas because when we broke up in the summer her tummy could barely fit behind her desk. Her tummy could barely fit behind

1

her *smock*. You could see her tummy button through the material, like a giant press fastener.

When I was a very little kid I used to think that's how babies were born. They grew inside the mother and then when they were ready the mum pressed her tummy button and out they popped. I told Jo how I'd got it all sussed out. Don't laugh. I was *very* little. *Jo* laughed. 'Dream on, Charlie,' she said. 'If only it were that easy.'

That's my name, Charlie. OK, my full name is Charlotte Alice Katherine Enright, but nobody ever calls me that. Jo and Lisa and Angela and all the kids at school call me Charlie. Some of the boys call me Cake or Carrot Cake or Cakehole, but they're just morons, though they think they're dead original. (Note the initials of my name. Got it?) But right since I was born, all the way through nursery and primary, no-one's ever called me Charlotte. Until this new teacher.

Miss Beckworth. She was new so I thought she'd be young. When you get a new young teacher they're often ever so strict the first few weeks just to show you who's boss, and then they relax and get all friendly. Then you can muck about and do whatever you want.

I *love* mucking about, doing daft things and being a bit cheeky and making everyone laugh. Even the teachers. But the moment I set eyes on Miss Beckworth I knew none of us were going to be laughing. She might be new but she certainly wasn't young. She had grey hair and grey eyes and a grey

2

and white blouse and a grey skirt and laced-up shoes, with a laced-up expression on her face to match. When she spoke her teeth were quite big and stuck out a bit, but I put all thought of Bugs Bunny imitations right out of my head.

There are some teachers – just a few – who have YOU'D BETTER NOT MESS WITH ME! tattooed right across their foreheads. She frowned at me with this incredibly fierce forehead and said, 'Good morning. This isn't a very good start to the new school year.'

Miss Beckworth

I stared at her. What was she on about? Why was she looking at her watch? I wasn't late. OK, the school bell had gone as I was crossing the playground, but you always get five minutes to get to your classroom.

'It's three minutes past nine,' Miss Beckworth announced. 'You're late.'

'No, I'm not,' I said. 'We're not counted late until it's five past.'

I didn't say it cheekily. I was perfectly polite. I was trying to be helpful, actually.

'You're *certainly* not off to a good start,' she goes. 'First you're late. And then you argue. My name's Miss Beckworth. What's your name?'

'Charlie, Miss Beckworth.' (See, *ever* so polite – because I could see I had to proceed d-e-l-i-c-a-t-e-l-y.)

'Your proper name?'

'Charlie Enright.'

'We don't seem to be connecting correctly, Miss Enright. Charlie isn't a proper name. It's a diminutive.'

She was trying to make *me* look pretty diminutive, obviously. I tried to act cool but I could feel my cheeks flushing. I have this very white skin that can be a real problem when I get mad or embarrassed. When you have a lot of long red hair and you get a red face too you start to look as if someone's put a match to you.

'Are you *Charles* Enright?'

I can't *stand* it when teachers go all sarcastic on you. A few of the kids tittered nervously. That posh prat Jamie laughed out loud. Typical. Angela and Lisa were looking all anguished, dying for me.

'I'm Charlotte Enright, Miss Beckworth. But I've never been called Charlotte at this school, only Charlie.'

'Well, I'm going to call you Charlotte, Charlotte. Because in my class we do things differently,' said Miss Beckworth.

You're telling me we do things differently. (Well, *I'm* telling *you*, but you know what I mean!) I wasn't allowed to go and sit with Angela. She'd promised to get to school ever so early to grab the best desk (and the one next to it for Lisa) and she'd done well. The desk right next to the window, with the hot pipe to toast my toes on when it got chilly. But all in vain.

'No, don't go and sit down, Charlotte,' said Miss Beckworth. 'I was just about to explain to the whole class that while we get to know each other I'd like

4

you all to sit in alphabetical order.'

We stared at her, gob-smacked.

Miss Beckworth spoke into the stunned silence, holding her register aloft.

'So, Anthony Andrews, you come and sit at this desk in the front, with Judith Ashwell beside you, and then—'

'But Judith's a girl, Miss!' Anthony protested in horror.

'Cleverly observed, Mr Andrews,' said Miss Beckworth. 'And kindly note, I call you Mr Andrews, not plain Mister. I would prefer you to call me Miss Beckworth. Not Miss.'

'But boys and girls never sit next to each other, Miss,' said Anthony. He's as thick as two short planks – *twenty*-two – but when Miss Beckworth's forehead wrinkled he rewound her little speech inside his empty head and took heed. 'Er, Miss Beckworth, Miss. I don't want to sit next to Judith!'

'Well, you needn't think I want to sit next to *you*,' said Judith. 'Oh Miss Beckworth, that's not fair!'

Miss Beckworth didn't care. 'I said things would be different in my class. I didn't say they would be fair,' she said. 'Now, get yourselves sorted out and stop fussing like a lot of silly babies. Who's next on the register? Laura Bernard, right, sit at the desk behind Anthony and Judith, and then . . .'

I hovered, signalling wild regret with my eyebrows to Angela, who'd got up half an hour early for nothing. Angela's surname is Robinson, so obviously we wouldn't sit together. But Lisa is Lisa Field, right after me on the register, so it looked as if we were OK after all. It wasn't really fair on poor Angela if I sat next to Lisa two years running, but it couldn't be helped.

But it didn't work out like that.

'James Edwards, you sit at the desk at the back on the left,' said Miss Beckworth. 'With . . . ah, Charlotte Enright beside you.'

Jamie Edwards! The most revolting stuck-up boring boy in the whole class. The whole year, the whole school, the whole town, county, country, world, *universe*. I'd sooner squat in the stationery cupboard than sit next to him.

I thought quickly, my brain going whizz, flash, bang. Aha! Sudden inspiration!

'I'm afraid I can't see very well, Miss Beckworth,' I said, squinting up my eyes as if I badly needed glasses. 'If I sit at the back I won't be able to see the board. Sometimes I still have problems even at the front – so if Lisa Field can come and sit next to me again, then I'm used to her telling me stuff in case I can't read it for myself. Isn't that right, Lisa?'

This was all news to Lisa, but she nodded convincingly.

'Yes, Miss Beckworth, I always have to help Charlie,' said Lisa.

But Miss Beckworth wasn't fooled. 'I'm not convinced that you're short-sighted, Charlotte. Quick-witted, certainly. But until you bring me a note from your mother and another from your

6

optician I'd like you to sit at the back beside James.'

That was it. I was doomed. There was no way out. I had to sit next to Jamie Edwards.

He moved his chair right up against the wall and shuddered elaborately as I flopped down furiously beside him.

'Charlie Cakehole! Yuck!' he said. But under his breath, because he knew Miss Beckworth was watching.

Jamie Edwards is the smarmiest little swot, and always wants the teachers to have him as their pet. Which he is anyway. Because he's such an infuriating Clever Clogs, always coming top top top.

Well, who on earth wants to be top of the class?

'Why can't you try harder at school, Charlie,' Jo always says. 'You're bright. If you'd only stop messing about and work hard you could do really well. You could come top if you really tried.'

I asked Jo why she always nagged so about my boring old education.

'Maybe you're not so bright as I thought you were,' Jo said. 'Can't you work it out for yourself?'

That made me feel bad. But it's hopeless. Maybe I could do better. I'm not bottom of the class, mind you. Just a nice comfy middle. But I suppose if I worked like stink then I could do better. I can generally beat Lisa and Angela if I want. Maybe I could come top of all the girls. But I couldn't ever beat Jamie Edwards. And I'd far sooner be bottom than second to Smarty Pants.

So I slid down in my seat and sulked for most of

Ooh! Please Miss Beckworth!

the morning. It was hot but Jamie kept me well-fanned, waving his hand frantically all the time because he kept wanting Miss Beckworth to pick him. Pathetic. I wouldn't put my hand up even when I knew the answers. Even in English, which is my best subject. I've always got ticks and stars and *Very Goods* all over the place for my stories.

Miss Beckworth started a poetry lesson and it was actually quite interesting and then she read this poem by some dippy American lady and you had to guess what it was about. Like a riddle. And no-one knew. Jamie guessed it might be about a river and Miss Beckworth said it was a very good guess – but it was wrong. Ha. *I* knew what it was. Easy-peasy, simple-pimple. It was a train. And I sat there with this pleased feeling throbbing through me, though I acted all cool and bored, slumped in my seat, arms folded . . . waiting. Waiting until she was just about to give up and then I was going to put my hand up after all and maybe yawn a bit or fiddle with my hair and then I was going to go 'It's a train' like it must be obvious to everyone. One up to me. And ya boo sucks to Jamie.

'Think really hard,' said Miss Beckworth. 'Can't anyone guess?'

And she looked straight at me, almost as if she could see inside my head and look at the train going puff puff puff round my brain.

I still waited. I waited just a fraction too long.

Because she stopped looking at me, and just as I was unfolding my arms ready to put my hand up she said, 'It's a train!'

And everyone else said, 'Oh, a train', 'Of course', '*I* get it', and Anthony and those of his ilk scratched their heads and said, 'You what?' and 'Why is it a train?' and 'I hate this soppy poem stuff.' I drummed my fingers on the desk in irritation and muttered, 'I knew it was a train.'

Jamie looked at me with those snooty eyebrows of his disappearing right up under his floppy fringe. 'Oh, sure,' he said sarcastically.

Well, I wouldn't have believed me either. But I *did* know. So I felt even less like joining in now and I drew trains all over the back of my new school jotter – large looming trains about to mash and mangle small snobby boys tied to the railway tracks.

Then we had to write our own poem about trains. I can usually write poems quite quickly so I did a silly one first on a piece of paper torn out of my jotter.

Puff puff puff
Can't stand
    this stuff
All about Trains
It gives me Pains
(Prize Pain to me
is Jamie E)

Help!

9

And Miss B is a Bore
Her train theme's a chore
Want to sit with my friend
I'm going round the bend
I feel so Blue
Choo choo choo!

I folded it up and put TO ANGELA AND LISA –
PASS IT ON – and then quickly passed it on myself
while Miss Beckworth's head was turned. It got
about halfway across the class. Miss Beckworth
looked up at the wrong moment. Uh-oh.

'Ah!' said Miss Beckworth, pouncing. 'Someone
has written a poem already, and they're so proud of
it they want to pass it round the whole class.'

She glanced at it. 'Who is the author of this little
rhyme, hmm?'

I put my hand up. I had to. Half the kids were
craning round to look at me already.

I thought I might be in dead trouble. Miss
Beckworth was such a funny old-fashioned teacher.
I didn't know what she might do to punish you.
Maybe she had a cane tucked up her skirt and she'd
whip it out and whack me one.

But all she did was crumple up my poem and say,
'I don't think this is quite Emily Dickinson standard,
Charlotte. Now write me a proper poem please.'

I decided she maybe wasn't such a bad old stick
after all – so I tried hard with my poem. I decided to
be a bit different. I chose to write about a tube,
because they're underground trains, aren't they,

and it was all about the dark in the tunnels and how that weird voice that says 'Mind the gap' could be the voice of the Tunnel Monster.

Jamie peered rudely over my shoulder. 'You're writing rubbish,' he sneered.

'Yours is the real rubbish,' I snapped back, reading his pathetic twee twoddle about the Train going through the Rain, in the Midst of the Storm, the Train will keep you Warm . . . Yuck!

But when Miss Beckworth walked round the class to see what we'd written so far she said he'd made a Good Attempt. And do you know what she said about *my* poem?

'Try to stick to the subject, Charlotte.'

That was *it*!

'Told you you were writing rubbish,' said Jamie.

So I put down my pen and didn't write another word. I had Angela and Lisa and all the other girls in hysterics in the cloakrooms after lunch doing my Miss Beckworth imitation. Even back in class I just had to put my front teeth over my bottom lip to have all the girls in giggles.

'Settle down, please,' said Miss Beckworth sharply. 'Now, History. I thought this term we'd do the Victorians.'

I ask you! Who wants to study the stuffy old Victorians? Well, guess. Jamie Teacher's Pet Edwards.

Miss Beckworth began telling us about the Victorians, starting off with Queen Victoria herself – that fat little waddly Queen with the pudding face

Queen Victoria

who said, 'We are not amused.' Well, I wasn't amused either, especially when Miss Beckworth started on about the Queen Vic pub down the road and Albert Park and how she lived in these old Victorian mansion flats, and did any of us live in a Victorian home by any chance?

I slumped to one side with the boredom of all this just as Jamie stuck his hand up so violently I *very* nearly got two fingers impaled up my nostrils.

'I live in a Victorian house, Miss Beckworth,' he said, showing off like mad. 'In Oxford Terrace.'

I sat up straight. I knew he was a right little posh nob – but I had no idea he lived in one of those huge grand houses in Oxford Terrace, all steps and little lion statues and incy-wincy balconies as if the people who live there might come and do a Royal Family and wave down at you.

Oxford Terrace is on our way home from the town. Sometimes when Jo and I are trailing back with our Sainsbury's bags cutting grooves in our hands we make up stuff and we sometimes play we live in Oxford Terrace and we're Lady Jo and Lady Charlie and we have champagne for breakfast and we go for a workout in a posh club every day and then we have a light lunch some-place snobby and then we shop until we drop, going flash flash flash with our credit cards, and then we eat out

Oxford Terrace. Wow!

and go dancing in nightclubs and chat up film stars and rock stars and football players but we just tease them and then jump into our personal stretch limousine and whizz home to our five-storey half-million mini-palace in Oxford Terrace.

'You live in Oxford Terrace???' I said.

Even Miss Beckworth seemed surprised. 'Do you live in a flat there, James?'

'No, we've got the whole house,' said Jamie airily.

'Well, perhaps you can help us understand what life was like in a big Victorian house, James.' Miss Beckworth rummaged amongst a whole box of books about the Victorians. She pounced on something about Victorian houses and held up a picture of a Victorian parlour. 'I don't suppose your house looks much like this inside, though, James?'

'Actually my mum and dad have this real thing about the Victorians and they've tried to make the house as authentic as possible, so we've got stuff like William Morris wallpaper and Arts and Crafts tiles – though we've got ordinary modern things like televisions and computers and stuff.'

I felt I was sitting next to Little Lord Fauntleroy. He carried on in this sickening fashion for ages until eventually even Miss Beckworth got tired of it.

'Thank you very much, James. If anyone wants to know more about Victorian houses then you're obviously a mine of information. Now, we'll be studying the Victorians all this term in class, but I want you all to work on your own special project at home too.'

I groaned. I hate home projects. 'You don't sound

ultra-enthusiastic, Charlotte,' said Miss Beckworth.

'Well. I don't know what to do. I don't know anything about the Victorians. Not like some people,' I said, glaring at Jamie.

'I'll copy a whole lot of suggestions for topics on the board. See if you can get your famously defective eyes to focus on them,' said Miss Beckworth briskly. 'It might be worth your while. I intend to award a prize for the best project at the end of term.'

So I copied out all her suggestions:

boring boring boring boring boring boring
boring HOME. FOOD. TOYS AND BOOKS. SCHOOL. boring
boring WORK. THE FAMILY. COURTSHIP. SUNDAY. boring
boring LAW AND ORDER. SEASIDE. CHRISTMAS. boring
boring boring boring boring boring boring boring

I didn't fancy any of them.

'Can we do more than one topic, Miss Beckworth,' said You-know-who. 'Can we do them *all* if we want?'

'Yes, if you like,' said Miss Beckworth.

He was quite sickening in his enthusiasm, grabbing all sorts of stuff from the book box, though he's probably got his own private library in his Victorian mansion.

'Here, it's not fair, you're bagging all the best books,' I said, trying to snatch at a book on Victorian hospitals that looked as if it might be promisingly gory.

'OK, OK. Here's one specially for you,' said Jamie – and he bungs me this book on Victorian domestic servants! 'Know your place,' he goes.

I was about to bash him on his big head with the servant book but Miss Beckworth got narky and told us to settle down and start the research for our projects with the books we had in our hands. So I was stuck with the servant book.

I flipped through it furiously – and then stopped. There was a photo of this girl about my age. She even looked a bit like me, skinny and pale. It was a black-and-white photo so it was hard to make out if her hair was red too. It was long, like mine, but scraped back tight behind her ears, with a little white cap crammed on top. She was surrounded by little kids, but they weren't her brothers and sisters. She was a nursery maid. She had to look after them. She was their servant.

I was a bit stunned. I didn't know they used to have children as servants. I read a bit about these nursery maids and kitchen maids and housemaids. They had to work all day and into the evening as well for hardly any money. Girls as young as eleven and twelve. No school. No play. No fun. Just work work work.

I decided I'd do a project on 'Servants'. I was all set to write quite a bit about it actually. I decided I'd show that Jamie.

But Jo was already at home when I got back from

school and she had such terrible scary news I forgot all about my servant project.

I didn't remember until the next day when everyone was showing off their project books. Jamie had done ten whole pages about 'School' and he'd stuck in this old photo of kids in rows in a Victorian classroom and got his mum to do some lines of special copperplate handwriting.

'I've finished my school topic already,' he boasted.

So I whipped out an old exercise book and scribbled out a page at playtime.

'I've finished my school topic too,' I said, sticking my tongue out at Jamie.

SCHOOL

My name is Lottie. I am eleven years old. I left school today.

My teacher, Miss Worthbeck, nearly cried when I told her I could not come back. She thinks the world of me. I am her most talented pupil. I am not being boastful, this is exactly what she said:

'Dear Lottie, you are the best at English and writing and arithmetic, you know your geography and history perfectly, you play the piano well, you paint beautifully and you sing like a lark.'

There! I am also useful to Miss Worthbeck, because she is the only teacher at our school, and she has to control a class of forty mixed infants and twelve of us older pupils. I am not the eldest by any means. There is one great lad of fourteen, Edward James, but he is very slow. He is a head taller than Miss Worthbeck, and she finds it hard to control this boy. In fact many of the boys are great lummoxes, stupid and surly. Miss Worthbeck has to use her cane on them to keep them in order.

Miss Worthbeck

Edward James

I do not need to resort to the cane when I am left in charge of the boys though I take delight in swishing it in front of them! But I usually instruct the little ones, and they all try hard for me and give me apples and bites of their gingerbread and scratch 'I love Lottie' on their slates.

Miss Worthbeck has always said I am a born teacher. She has always wanted me to stay on at the school until fourteen, and then she will give me a position as a pupil—teacher, with a proper wage. But I cannot wait two years. I need to earn a proper wage immediately.

HOME

Jo and I haven't always had a home. We lived with Grandma and Grandpa at first. That was pretty bad. Grandma is the sort of lady who keeps a damp flannel neatly folded in a plastic bag and she's forever whipping it out and smearing round imaginary sticky bits. On me. Even at my age. That's nothing. She does it to Jo too.

Keep still child!

She doesn't do it to Grandpa because he's one of those pale men in stripy suits who don't ever get sticky. I can't imagine hanging on to his sharply creased trousers or bouncing on his bony knees when I was a baby.

Grandma

Grandma and Grandpa didn't want Jo and me around, but we didn't have any place else to go. Then we got told about the Newborough Estate and asked if we wanted a flat there. Grandma and Grandpa just about died. You've probably not heard of the Newborough Estate unless you live around here. You'll *definitely* have heard of it if you do. The police

Grandpa

get called out every night. And the fire service, because the kids keep setting fire to the rubbish in the chutes. The ambulances are always there too, because there are so many fights and people getting battered. Sometimes they come to scrape up the bodies because people throw themselves off the balconies because they're so fed up living in a dump like the Newborough Estate.

But we went to live there, Jo and me. There was this HUGE row and Grandma and Grandpa said they were really washing their hands of us this time. But Jo stood up to them. Funny that. Jo can't say boo to a goose. She lets everyone walk all over her. Especially me.

Jo

She worries terribly about Grandma and Grandpa and she tries so hard to please them. When they come over nowadays and pick faults – Grandma's the worst, pick pick pick, and Jo winces like she's scraping at her actual skin – she still stands up to them over me. It's as if it's easy-peasy, simple-pimple where I'm concerned.

I asked her how come once.

'Because you mean more to me than anyone else,' said Jo.

She does to me too. She's my mum. You guessed that, didn't you? You wouldn't guess it though if you saw us out together. Big sister and little sister, that's what you'd think. With me the big sister. No, that's just a joke. Though it won't be long before I'm taller than her. She's only little and I'm getting big.

There's only that much in it now.

There's not much between us age-wise either. She was still at school when she had me. Shock Horror Disaster!

That's what Grandma and Grandpa thought. Of course, I wasn't observing much in those days but I can imagine it all too well. Jo's told me lots of stuff anyway. They didn't want her to have me. And then after I got born they wanted Jo to put me in a Home. The sort with a capital H. So that Jo could start a new life all over again.

'This is my new life,' said Jo. 'As if I'd ever give my baby away! I'll make a proper home for both of us.'

She did too. It wasn't so bad on the Newborough Estate. Well, it was some of the time. Like when we got our door kicked in and boys wrote stuff all over the walls. Or the day this loony cornered us in the lift. Or the time our telly got nicked the day after it got delivered.

But we made some great friends there too.

It was our home, even though we didn't have any cash to do it up and make it look pretty. We were on benefit at first, and then Jo got a job once she'd got me into nursery, but we didn't spend much even then. We were saving.

Grandma and Grandpa stopped being so huffy and offered us lots of money to get us out of the Newborough Estate. I thought Jo was mad to say no. But she said we had to do it all by ourselves. To show them. Because they didn't think we stood a chance.

But we made it! Jo worked hard at her job selling televisions and washing machines and we saved like crazy and then Jo got a promotion and another and then guess what. She was made the manageress of the big branch down in the shopping centre, in charge of a staff of twelve. And so we started hanging out around estate agent windows, looking for anything going really cheap because people keep getting made redundant in our area and so they can't keep up the payments on their homes and they get taken away from them.

There were a few ex-council flats we could have managed, posher than the Newborough Estate, but Jo wasn't having that.

'We want something Private,' she said. 'Small but select.'

And that's what we've got. A one-bedroomed flat in a quiet private block with laid-out gardens. No-one tore out the roses or smashed the windows or peed in the lift. The people living there were mostly elderly ladies or young married couples or schoolteachers who don't usually tear and smash and pee publicly. They looked a bit nervously at Jo and me when we moved in – especially me – but Jo insisted we had to be on our Best Behaviour at all times.

'Well, at least till we get accepted,' she said. 'So we'll keep the CD player turned down *low*, right, and we'll smile at everyone and say stuff like Good Morning and Good Afternoon ever so polite and we won't go barging straight past someone to get in the lift first and if we're having one of our famous ding-dong rows we'll have to do it in a whisper, get it?'

I got it. I stuck to all these rules. Most of the time. And we've *got* accepted. Oh, one or two of the truly stuffy old bags have asked me pointed questions about Daddy and then they mumble with raised eyebrows, but even those ones say hello and offer me toffees and tell me how tall I'm getting. We're friends with just about everyone in the flats.

But we don't really need all the other people, of course. When we shut our blue front door (I wanted red, but Jo said we had to blend in with the others along the balcony) then we're home and it's all ours and we can be our family. Small, but select, like the flats.

We still haven't got much money to do it all up because most of Jo's earnings go on the mortgage. We've got a good telly and video and CD player and washing machine though (because Jo gets them at a serious discount) and we've painted all the flat so that it looks great. Jo wanted white for the living room (boring) but she let me choose this amazing dark red for our bedroom, and we've got these truly wonderful crimson curtains we found at a boot fair and a deep purply-red lamp and when it's a treat day like a birthday we draw the curtains and switch on the lamp and have a special red picnic in our beautiful bright bedroom. Cherries, plums, jam tarts, strawberry split ice creams, Ribena for me and red wine for Jo, yum yum.

I was kind of hoping Jo and me might be having a bedroom picnic that evening because she had an appointment with the manager for the whole of our area and she was hoping it might be about further promotion.

It was scary opening the door of our flat and seeing Jo because she doesn't usually get back from work till six at the earliest. But there she was, sitting in the middle of the living-room floor. Not doing anything, just sitting with her hands clasped round her knees.

'Jo? What's up?' She looked so small sitting there like that. I towered over her as I stood beside her. 'Jo, why are you home from work? Don't you feel well? Have you been sick?' I thought maybe that was it. She looked so white. No, *grey*, and her eyes were all watery.

'Oh, Charlie,' she whispered.
'*What?*'

'The most terrible thing's happened,' she said in such a tiny voice that I had to bend right down close to hear.

All these different possibilities came bubbling up inside my head until I felt as if it was boiling. 'Tell me,' I said.

Jo opened her mouth again but her voice was just a wisp now.

'*Tell* me, go on. You're scaring me,' I said, giving her shoulder a little shake.

I could feel she was shivering even though it was hot in the flat and she hadn't bothered to open any of the windows when she came in.

'Jo?' I sat down properly beside her and put my arm right round her.

She gave a little stifled sound and then tears started dribbling down her face.

'It can't be that bad, whatever it is,' I said desperately. 'We've still got each other and our flat and—'

'We haven't!' Jo sobbed. 'Well, we've got each other. But we won't be able to keep the flat. Because I've lost my job.'

'What? But that's ridiculous! You're great at your job. They think the world of you. How could they get rid of you? Was this the area manager? Is he crazy?'

'He's lost his job too. We all have. The firm's closing down. We all knew things had been a bit tight recently, and some of the smaller shops closed, but no-one thought . . . They've just gone bust, Charlie. They can't find a buyer so that's it. They've ordered us to lock up all the shops. I'm out of a job.'

'Well . . . you'll get another one. Easy-peasy, simple-pimple,' I said.

'I wish you wouldn't keep saying that,' said Jo, sniffing. 'It sounds so stupid. And you're being stupid. How am I going to get another job? All the electrical goods chains are struggling. There's no jobs going there. I've been to the Job Centre. There's nothing going in retail at all. There's some office work, but they want all sorts of GCSEs and certificates. Which I haven't got, have I? I'm the one that's stupid.'

'No you're not,' I said. Even though she'd just said I was stupid.

'I should have tried to keep up with my school-work. Gone to evening classes,' Jo wept.

'You had me.'

'I could have been catching up these last few years. But I didn't think I needed to. I was doing so well at work . . .'

'You'll get another job, Jo, honest you will. There *must* be shop jobs going somewhere. You'll get a job easy . . . You'll get a job, I promise.'

I promised until I was blue in the face but of course we both knew I could turn positively navy but it wouldn't make any difference.

Jo didn't come to bed till very late that night and then she didn't sleep for ages. She tried not to toss and turn but whenever I woke up I knew immediately she was awake. Lying stiff and still, staring up at our crimson ceiling. Only it doesn't look red at night. It's black in the dark.

I woke up very early, long before the alarm. At least the ceiling was dimly red now. Jo was properly asleep at last, her hair all sticking up, her mouth slightly open. She had one hand up near her face, clenched in a fist. I propped myself up on one elbow, watching her for a bit, and then I slid out of bed.

Jo won't let me stick any posters or magazine pictures up in the living room. We've got a proper print of a plump lady cuddling her daughter with a white frame to match the walls. I didn't want to mess up the round red glow of the bedroom but I've stuck up heaps and heaps of stuff in the loo. Want to see?

Of course, it's a bit weird with all these eyes watching you when you go to the toilet. Lisa and Angela always have a giggle about it when they come to my place.

They both like my home a lot. They've got much bigger houses but they think mine's best. They're thrilled if I ever have one or other of them to stay over. (They have to come separately – and even then Jo has to sleep on the sofa in the living room.)

Angela's house seems quite small too but that's just because she's got a big family, not just brothers and sisters but a granny and an auntie or two. It's fun at Angela's house and she's got a super mum who

laughs a lot and she cooks amazing food. Angela and I stayed up half Saturday night and got the giggles so bad when we went to bed that we still couldn't get to sleep for ages. I nearly fell asleep in church. That's the disadvantage of staying over at Angela's. We went to church *twice* on Sunday. I might even have had to go *again* in the evening if Jo hadn't picked me up in time.

Lisa's got an even bigger home with a huge garden and a swing. We put up this tent in her garden and camped out in it, though I'd have sooner slept in her bedroom which is pink and white and ever so pretty, with special twin beds with pink and white flowery duvets. Lisa's mum is all pink and white too and she smells very flowery but she isn't always as soft and gentle as she looks. She nags Lisa about all sorts of stuff. But Lisa's dad adores her. He calls her his little Lisalot and when he comes home from work he gives her such a big hug he lifts her right off her feet.

Lisa said it must be awful for me not having a dad. I said I didn't care a bit. And I don't. I've got Jo.

Sometimes Jo and I play this silly game that we're both male, because we've both got funny names. I'm little-boy Charlie and she's this big gruff funny bloke Jo who's my dad. We often have games together where we muck around and play at being different people. When I was little my favourite game of all was me being Jo and Jo being me, so that I was the mother and got to tell her what to do.

I wandered out of the loo and into the living room and stared at the space on the carpet where Jo had sat yesterday. I felt as if I was the mother now and she was the little kid – but it wasn't a game.

The minute Jo woke up she said, 'What are we going to do?' As if *I* knew.

I felt worried about leaving her at home when I went to school. I kept wondering if she was sitting on the living-room floor again, all hunched up. I was thinking about Jo and her job and our home so much I didn't listen in lessons and Miss Beckworth got really narked with me. So I acted cheeky and then I was in serious trouble, but I didn't really mind. That just made things more normal.

Miss Beckworth kept me in at dinner time. She didn't give me any stupid lines to write out, though. She said I could work on my Victorian project.

Boring boring boring, I thought – but better than lines. And at least I had the book box to myself. I asked for something about Victorian homes.

'Not a posh house for the rich. What about an ordinary little home for a poor family? Aren't there any books about that?'

She found me one or two pages, but there wasn't much. So I made a lot of it up.

HOME

There is nothing for it. I have to leave home.

I love my home very much, although it is only a tumbledown cottage, stifling hot in the summer and bitter cold in winter. The winters have always been the worst. Two little brothers and one infant sister died during the winter months, and Father passed away last February when the snow was thick on the ground.

I did not cry when Father died. Perhaps it is wicked to admit this, but I felt relieved. He treated Mother very bad, and though he earned a fair wage he drank a great deal of it. So we were always poor even then, but Mother kept our simple home shining bright. She made bright rag rugs to cover the cold stone flags of the floor and each bed upstairs had a pretty patchwork quilt. I cut out pictures from the illustrated papers and pinned them to the walls. I even pinned pictures out in the privy!

There was always a rabbit stew bubbling on the black–

Jessie Me Rose Frank Mother
and Ada-May

leaded range when we came home from school.
We'd dig potatoes or carrots or cabbage from the
garden, and in the summer Rose and Jessie and I
would pick a big bunch of flowers to go in the pink
jug Frank won at the fair.

Mother always liked us to wash our hands and
say Grace at the table before eating. Father never
washed his hands or said Grace, but Mother could
do nothing about that. Sometimes Father did not
come home until very late. One night last winter he
fell coming home in the dark and lay where he
was till morning. They carried him home to us and
Mother nursed him night and day but the cold got
to his chest.

Mother used up her sockful of savings on
Father's funeral. She bought us all a set of black
mourning clothes, even little Ada-May. I thought
this a waste of money, but Mother is determined
that we stay respectable.

Our grandmother and grandfather did not want
Mother to marry Father. They thought he was a
wastrel, far too fond of the Demon
Drink. I privately agreed, but I did
not like them saying this to Mother.
They came to Father's funeral
and said it all over again. They
asked Mother how she was
going to manage now.

Mother said she would
take in washing and do fine
sewing for ladies.

Grandmother

Grandfather

Grandmother and Grandfather sniffed. They took a shine to my sister Rose, who is pretty, and offered her a home with them. It will be one mouth less for you to feed, they said. Mother asked Rose if she wanted to live with Grandmother and Grandfather and she cried and said no. So Mother said we would all stick together.

'You will be sticking together in the Workhouse then,' said Grandmother.

Mother stuck her chin in the air and said we would manage fine. But I heard her crying at night. I went to comfort her. 'We will manage fine, Mother, you'll see,' I said.

But it has become very hard. Mother washes all day and sews half the night. She has become very pale and thin and coughs a good deal. I am very frightened that she will get really ill in the winter if she keeps working so hard. Frank and Rose and I tried to help out this spring and summer, running errands and selling nosegays and sweet lemonade at the market. But we can only earn pennies. We need pounds to keep us out of the workhouse.

So it is up to me. I am the oldest. I must go and earn money and send it to Mother. There is only one job a girl my age can go for. I must be a servant.

WORK

The phone rang. I answered it automatically. Lisa and Angela are always ringing me up – and some of the other girls in our class. I don't want to sound disgustingly boastful but I am quite popular.

But it wasn't a girl. It was Grandma.

'Hello, Charlotte dear,' said Grandma.

I told a teeny white lie to Miss Beckworth. Grandma always calls me Charlotte, pursing her lips and clicking her teeth. If you're standing right in front of her you get sprayed with spit. I found I was holding the telephone at arm's length just in case.

'Can I speak to Mummy, please?' said Grandma.

That's another weird thing she does. I've never called Jo Mummy in my life. But Grandma always does. As if Jo is *her* Mummy. Though Grandma treats Jo as if she's a silly little toddler, not a grown-up woman with a practically grown-up daughter of her own.

Grandma's voice is so loud it boomed right across the room to Jo. She shook her head in a panic. 'Say I'm not here!' she mouthed at me.

She'd been crying and she'd got to that sodden stage where everything is still dribbling. She

33

fumbled for a tissue and blew her nose dolefully.

'I'm afraid Jo's just nipped out to the shops, Grandma,' I lied.

'Don't be silly, Charlotte. It's half past seven in the evening,' Grandma said briskly.

'There's heaps of shops still open round here, Grandma. There's the video shop, and the off-licence, and the Spar down the road—'

Grandma gave a disdainful snort. 'Please don't argue with me, Charlotte. I know Mummy's there, I can hear her blowing her nose. I want to talk to her.'

'Well, she doesn't want to talk to you,' I said – but in a little squeaky-mouse mumble as I passed the phone over.

'Josephine?'

'Hello, Mum,' said Jo wearily, sniffing.

'Are you crying?' Grandma demanded.

'No, I – of course I'm not crying,' said Jo, a tear dribbling down her cheek.

'Say you've got a cold!' I whispered, miming a major bout of sneezing.

'I've got a cold,' Jo said, nodding at me gratefully. 'Why on earth should I be crying?'

'Well, you tell me,' said Grandma. 'Your father's just read a most disturbing item on the financial page of his newspaper. It says Elete Electrical have folded.'

Jo shut her eyes and said nothing.

'Josephine? Are you still there? Is it true? Is it a

nationwide collapse? You are being kept on until they find a new buyer, aren't you? And if the worst comes to the worst, they will give you a substantial redundancy payment, won't they?'

Jo sniffed again but still couldn't speak.

'Do say something, dear,' said Grandma. 'We're very worried about you. We've always said you're in a very precarious position. How on earth are you going to keep up the payments on your flat if you lose your job? You and Charlotte can barely manage as it is. We do worry about you so.'

Jo opened her eyes. She stood up straight. She gave one last giant sniff and then spoke.

'Honestly, Mum, you do get into a silly state. There's no need to worry. We're fine. I feel I was ready for a change from Elete anyway. Of course I've known for a long time that things have been precarious with the firm – which is why I applied for my new job. I have this brilliant managerial position, and a much larger salary too – so Charlie and I are very comfortably off at the moment. I really must go now, Mum, I badly need to get a hankie, my goodness, this is a terrible cold, I think I'd better have an early night with honey and hot lemon, well, goodbye, thanks for phoning.'

She said this without pausing, absolutely gabbling the last bit and then slamming the phone down quick. Then she took the receiver off again, so that Grandma couldn't call back.

'What?' Jo said to me, wiping her cheeks with the cuff of her shirt.

'You know what! You told her one socking great lie,' I said admiringly.

'Well, I couldn't stand her going on and on like that.'

'But she'll find out that it's not true,' I said.

'I'm going to *make* it come true,' said Jo. 'You'll see.'

All the tight feeling in my tummy untwisted. It was OK. Of course Jo would get another job, easy-peasy, simple-pimple.

She was up early the next morning, hair washed, all made up, blouse fresh on, skirt carefully pressed. When I woke up she was walking up and down the bedroom, practising.

'Good morning. My name's Jo Enright. I've been the manageress of a large shop for the last year but now I feel it's time for a change. Are there any new job opportunities in your company?' she asked our bedroom wardrobe, shaking the sleeve of her dressing gown.

'Good morning. I am Mr Wardrobe. Yes, Ms Enright, you can come and manage my clothes for me and I'll pay you a million pounds a week,' I said from under the covers.

'Charlie! You didn't half give me a fright!' said Jo, finding my tummy through the duvet and tickling it.

'Don't make me laugh! I need to go to the loo. I'll wet the bed, I'm warning you,' I giggled, rolling around.

'Well, get up and go, you lazy thing,' said Jo, trying to tip me out. 'Come on, you'll be late for school. And I thought this new teacher of yours is dead strict?'

'You're telling me! Lisa and Angela and me didn't feel like playing boring old rounders yesterday so we hid in the girls' toilets. We've done that heaps of times and no-one ever thought a thing about it before, but Miss Beckworth came looking for us, right into the toilets, and when we all hid in a cubicle she peered underneath the door and said, "Will the girl with six feet please come out of this toilet immediately." We thought we were really in for it, but she said she'd hated games at school too and as she'd already picked the two rounders teams we didn't have to play just this one time and we thought *great* – but do you know what we had to do instead? Run round and round the play-ground without stopping for the entire lesson. We were absolutely *knack-ered*. And every time we ran past her and begged for mercy she said brightly, "Aren't you lucky to be taking part in *my* rounders game, girls?" She's so . . . slippery. You can't suss out what she's going to do next. Every time you get ready to hate her she's funny and then when you start to think she's an old softie she plays a trick on you.' I was in the bathroom by this time, sitting on the loo.

'She sounds a good teacher,' Jo called. She

followed me into the bathroom. 'Do you think I look a bit older and more professional with my hair up? Yeah, I think so. Help me pin it up at the back, eh?'

She's usually great at fixing her own hair but her hands were all fumbly this morning, and she couldn't eat any breakfast because she said she was too nervous.

'You've got to eat something. You don't want to faint dramatically in the middle of a job interview,' I said.

'Maybe I won't *get* any interviews,' Jo said. Then she stopped and took a deep breath. 'No. I've got to think positive. Right, Charlie?'

'You bet. Good luck, Jo,' I said, hugging her.

I hoped and hoped Jo would get a job that day. She went into town and she walked round in her high heels with this big bright smile on her face, going into all these different shops and introducing herself and asking and then nodding and walking out again, over and over, all day long. She came home and she kicked her shoes off and she howled. But then I made her a cup of tea and rubbed her feet and she stopped crying and the next day she tried again. And the next.

A shop selling weird way-out clothes was advertising for staff but they said Jo wasn't wacky enough. A big store wanted a sales assistant for their ladies' dress department but they said Jo wasn't mature enough. A snobby shop selling designer clothes made it plain Jo wasn't posh enough.

'This is hopeless,' said Jo, sighing.

She tried record shops, but she didn't know enough about modern music. She'd been too busy bringing me up to dash down the disco. She tried bookshops, because she likes reading,

Not wacky enough
Not mature enough
Not cool enough
Not posh enough
Not studenty enough

but the only shop with a vacancy was full of all these student boys in jeans making jokey remarks, and the one with the scruffiest hair and the grubbiest T-shirt turned out to be the manager and although Jo said he was friendly it was obvious she didn't fit.

She charged out at seven in the morning on Friday to buy the local paper and she skimmed through all the small print looking for jobs.

'Nothing!' she said despairingly. 'Well, no proper jobs. There's bar work. But I'm not leaving you alone in the evenings.'

'Don't be daft. I'll be fine. Go for it, Jo! You could learn how to make all those great cocktails with the little cherries and toy umbrellas. It would be fun,' I said.

Jo went to the pub to see what it was like.

'It would not be fun,' she said. 'I wouldn't be making any cocktails there. Just serving pints of bitter to a lot of boring old men trying to look down my front. I could put up with that, but I wouldn't be free till half past eleven every night and then I'd have to walk miles home unless I forked out for a taxi – and they were only paying fifty pounds for five full evening shifts. We can't pay the mortgage with that.'

Jo went back to the local paper. 'The only other jobs are cleaning,' she said.

'What do you mean, cleaning? Like at Sketchley's?' I said.

'No, not a dry cleaning shop. Cleaning ladies. You know.'

I looked at Jo.

'I can clean, can't I?' she said.

'But you hate cleaning. Look at all the fights we have over whose turn it is to vacuum.'

'OK, OK. But this is in a supermarket. You get socking great industrial cleaning machines. I quite fancy charging about with one of those.'

She didn't mean it, of course. She was just being brave.

'It's two hours every morning, that's all. Sixty-two pounds,' said Jo, tearing out the advert.

'That's not enough to pay the mortgage.'

'I know. But look, there are heaps of other adverts for cleaners. I could go after them too. Listen. "Private house, cleaning, some ironing, nine to twelve, Mondays and Thursdays, thirty pounds". And then there's this one here, they want two hours' cleaning daily plus someone to look after a little boy after school.'

'You don't want to be lumbered with someone else's little *boy*,' I said.

'I don't want to be lumbered with my own great

big girl if she's going to be so picky,' said Jo. 'Look, Charlie. I haven't got any choice. I'll keep on trying to get a proper job but until that happens I might as well earn what I can. It's lousy money but it all adds up. So shut up about it, OK?'

I shut up. Jo phoned the supermarket and they told her to come along for an interview. She rushed off. I sat by myself, feeling fidgety. Then I got out my notepad and a big fat felt tip pen. I wrote out my own advert.

STRONG RELIABLE SCHOOLGIRL
WANTS WORK. WILL DO SHOPPING,
RUN ERRANDS, WHATEVER YOU WANT.
APPLY MISS C. A. K. ENRIGHT,
NO. 38 MEADOWBANK.

WORK

I've got work. I earn eleven pounds a year. One pound for every year of my age.

I did not tell anyone my real age. I swore I was thirteen, going on fourteen. I do not know whether anyone believed me. I put my hair up and lowered the hem of my skirt as far as it would go. At least I looked respectable in my mourning clothes.

I went to a domestic service agency in town. They said they had just the job for me. But when I went to the house and saw the cross sulky face of the Mistress I wasn't so sure. I did not find out what the Master did for a living, but it was easy to tell he was not a gentleman. They wanted a maid-of-all-work and I could see at once I'd be toiling all day long and well into the night, and scolded all the time no matter what pains I took. I am willing to be a servant but I will not be a slave.

I went back to the agency and said the first position wasn't suitable. They seemed astonished at my effrontery, but sent me after another position. I thought at first this was more likely. It was in a grand house with six servants. I was to be the nursery maid, helping the upper-nurse care for a little boy.

I do not care for little boys. My brother Frank has always been a great trial to me. I believe he takes after Father. I certainly did not care for this little boy, who stuck out his tongue in a very rude manner and then kicked me hard upon the shin. I did not care for the upper-nurse either, who had a face like a boot and long nipping fingers like button hooks. But I would have taken the position even so, if it weren't for the Master of the house. He was a widower, and I was all prepared to feel sorry for him if he were still mourning his late wife. Ha!

This gentleman patted me at the interview and said I was a fine-looking girl fresh from the country. His eyes slid sideways and I detested the way he was looking at me. He might be a gentleman but he didn't act like one. I knew he would be quick to take liberties and if I complained I would be sent packing with no reference. I am young but I am no fool.

I went back to the agency yet again and said the second position wasn't suitable either, and I said why, too. This time they were appalled at my impertinence. How dare I criticize my Betters? But

they gave me one last chance. I knew I had to
take it this time.

I do hope it is third time lucky. I am employed by
a mistress who wants a young nurse for her three
children, Victor who is six, Louisa who is four,
and baby Freddie who is still in petticoats. I did not meet the Master, but I
shall have to hope for the best. There
are two other servants in the household,
a cook and a housemaid. I hope they
will be friendly.

I am not sure about this mistress. She does not
look cross but she seems very firm. She told me
my duties in great detail. I must light the fires
when I get up and dust the day nursery, I must
dress Louisa and help Victor with his boots and
buttons, I must attend to the baby, and then we
have breakfast. Victor and Louisa are then to be
sent down to their mother while I wash and dress
baby Freddie and give him his bottle and put him
back in his cot. I must then clean and tidy the night
nursery and then dress the children in outdoor
clothes and take them for a walk. They will have
a rest on our return while I brush their clothes and
clean their boots, and then I must get them ready
for their dinner. We are to take another walk in
the afternoon when possible, and then after a light
tea I must put baby Freddie to bed while Victor
and Louisa go downstairs. Then I must put them
to bed and tidy the nurseries and eat my supper
and then go to bed myself.

'Do you feel you can manage all this?' she said. 'You look very little.'

'But I am strong, Madam. I will manage,' I said determinedly.

'Very good. You can start on Monday. I will give you the print for your uniform and a bolt of cotton for your apron and caps. I hope you are satisfactory at sewing, Charlotte?'

I blinked at her. 'Charlotte, Madam?' I said foolishly.

'That is your name, is it not?' she said.

'No, Madam. I am called Lottie, Madam. It was the name of Mother's doll when she was small. No—one's ever called me Charlotte.'

'Well, I do not think Lottie is a suitable name for a servant. You will be called Charlotte whilst you are working for me.'

FOOD

Jo phoned me from the town.

'Guess what! I've got the job.'

'Great!'

'Well. It's not really. It wasn't even a proper interview. It obviously doesn't matter what you're like when you're a cleaner.'

'Still. I bet you're going to be the best-ever squeakiest-cleanest cleaner they've ever had,' I said.

'The start of a whole new career,' said Jo. 'Do you think I'll make it to the Champion Floor Cleaning Polish trials, hmm?'

'You bet. So you'd better get into training quick. When do you start?'

'Tomorrow.' I heard Jo gulp. 'At six. In the morning. Oh, Charlie, I must be mad. I could claim income support and lie in bed till noon.'

'Still, you don't have to fib to Grandma any more. You really have got a job.'

'I can just imagine what she'll say when she finds out I'm a cleaner.'

'No, you're not a *cleaner*. You're . . . you're a state-of-the-floor supervisor, right?'

'You're a sweet kid, Charlie.'

'I was a snotty kid earlier. You coming home then? I'm starving.'

'Yes, I've just got to buy something for tea. I hoped I might get staff discount at this supermarket but that's only for the women working the tills.'

'Get some red treats for a bedroom picnic to celebrate your job.'

'Hey, we're economizing.'

'Very cheap red treats?'

'Do you think baked beans could be called red?'

'Just. Get some red plums for pudding.'

'Or red apples. And a block of raspberry ripple ice cream?'

'Yes! And what about a strawberry gâteau?'

'I think that's coming it a bit, old girl. Beans, plums and ice cream, that'll do. I'll be home soon then. You get the trays ready.'

I padded about the kitchen thinking we really should have a cake to celebrate properly. I remembered this ancient packet of cake mix I'd won on a tombola at the school fête donkey's years ago. I had a poke around the kitchen cupboard and found it crumpled behind some tins of soup. Jo didn't go in for making cakes and the only sort I'd ever made were pretend pink dough ones when I was a little kid, but this packet sort looked a doddle. You just had to add an egg. I found one egg in a box at the back of the fridge. I thought back to when we'd last had scrambled eggs and it was only about a fortnight ago so it should be all right.

I tipped the contents of the cake mix packet into

a bowl, swished the egg around until it was all sticky, scooped the lot into the tin and shoved it in the oven. Easy-peasy, simple-pimple.

'What's that lovely smell?' said Jo when she came in the door.

'A surprise. Hey, congratulations.'

'I've got *two* jobs! I phoned the number where they want someone to look after the little boy as well as do a bit of cleaning. That's in the afternoon, so it'll be easy to fit that in too.'

'Where are you going to look after this little boy then? Not round here, I hope,' I said. 'I don't want him messing up all my stuff.'

'He sounds a nice sensible little boy, though he's very shy. I spoke to him on the phone. And his dad sounds nice too, though ever so sad. His wife left and he's trying to cope on his own.'

'We cope fine on *our* own,' I said. 'Look, you're a cleaner now. Why don't you just stick to cleaning jobs. You don't want to be a nanny too.'

'It's seventy-five pounds a week. That's not bad. If I could find just one more job like that to fit in mid-morning then we'd be laughing,' said Jo. 'Hey, is your surprise all right? It's not burning, is it?'

It had burnt just a little bit, but only around the edges. I decided to cut them off – and then I went on cutting and trimming, turning the round sponge into two letters, a big 'J' and a small round circle for the 'o'. We didn't have any icing so I smeared some strawberry jam on the top and then studded both letters with Smarties.

'That looks wonderful,' said Jo. 'Hey, you're really good at this.'

I don't want to sound disgustingly boastful, but it really wasn't bad for a first attempt.

I added a line to my work advert:

MAKES EXCELLENT CAKES.

I didn't show Jo my advert. I wanted to surprise her. But when I took my advert into the newsagent's and asked Mr Raj to put it in the window he shook his head.

'You can't work. You're just a little girl,' he said.

'Girls work just as well as boys. *Better*,' I said indignantly.

'It's not because you're a girl. You're too young. You couldn't do any proper work.'

'Yes I could! Look, a hundred years ago I could work full time as someone's servant. I could be scrubbing all day. I'm doing this project about it for school, see.'

'That's what you should be doing at your age. Concentrating on your school work.'

'You don't get paid for doing school work.'

'You kids. Just wanting money money money. What do you want? A bike? Roller blades? A computer? My kids want all these things, nag nag nag. If the boy don't turn up to deliver the newspapers and I ask my boy to help me out then it's "How much money will you pay me?"'

'*I'll* do a newspaper round,' I said.

'You can't. You're too little. It's against the law, see. Times have moved on since your history project. Kids aren't allowed to work.'

I could see I was wasting my time. I tried the newsagent's down in the town but he said the same. So I decided to use my initiative. I'm quite good at that. I spent most of my spare cash photocopying my advert and then I went round sticking them through people's letterboxes in our flats and the flats over the road and half the houses down the street.

I'd put my phone number, so I sat by the phone and waited. And waited. And waited.

'What's up with you?' said Jo.

'Nothing.'

'Come on. Are you waiting for a phone call?'

'I might be.'

'Don't play games with me, Charlie, I'm feeling too dopey to work it out,' said Jo, yawning.

She'd started her job at the supermarket and was finding it an awful struggle to get out of bed at five.

'Look, why don't you go to bed now, get a really early night. You look exhausted,' I said.

'Why do you want me out the way? Who is it who's going to phone, eh?' Jo's sleepy eyes suddenly sparkled. 'Hey, it's a boy!'

'What?'

'You're waiting for some boy to phone you!'

'I am not.'

'Yes, you are. You've got a boyfriend,' said Jo, giggling.

'Don't be so stupid. I hate boys.'

'So you *say*. I know. It's . . . what's-his-name? The one you keep going on about at school. The one you sit next to.'

'Jamie Edwards! You have to be joking. I can't *stick* him. Sitting next to him is driving me absolutely crazy.'

I couldn't believe Jo could be so crackers. I truly detested that Jamie. He was just the most annoying person in the whole world to have to sit next to. He waved his hand in the air so often to answer Miss Beckworth's questions that I was in a permanent breeze. And every time he got the answer right – which was nearly flipping always – he gave this smug satisfied little nod, as if to say, see, what a super intelligent smartie-boots I am.

I hated the way when Miss Beckworth set us some work he'd start straight away, his posh fountain pen bobbing up and down as he wrote, while the rest of us were still scratching our heads and ruling margins and looking at our watches to see how long it was till playtime.

I hated the way his work came back from Miss Beckworth, tick tick tick at every paragraph, and *Well done, Jamie!* written at the bottom. I got lots of crosses and *You could try much harder, Charlotte,* and *Tut tut, this is very shoddy work,* and *You can't fool me by making your writing enormous and widely spaced. You can only have spent five minutes on this work at the most. This is not good enough!*

I didn't want to be bothered with anything else but learning about the Victorians. I was starting to kind of enjoy writing my project. It was weird. I read stuff in books and then started writing and it was as if this other girl entirely was scribbling it all down. The servant girl. Lottie the nursery maid. She'd started to feel real, like I'd known her all my life. I knew her better than I even knew Lisa or Angela. I just picked up a pencil and all *her* thoughts came rushing out on the paper.

I couldn't stand the thought of Miss Beckworth speckling it with her red biro. It was private. At least we didn't have to hand our projects in till they were finished, and we had weeks yet.

Of course You-know-who had practically finished his project already. He didn't want to keep *his* project private. He kept flashing it around at every opportunity. He even took it into the canteen with him at dinner time. Well, he did that once. I just happened to choke on a fishfinger and so needed an immediate drink of Coke and in my haste I happened to tip the can over and the merest little spitty bit of froth spattered Jamie's precious folder. Only the outside. But he declared the posh marbled paper was all spoilt. The next day he carted his project to school, completely re-covered with repro-Victorian wrapping paper, all fat frilly girls in bonnets and soppy boys in sailor suits, yuck yuck. And inside there was page after page of Jamie's neat blue handwriting with his own elaborate illustrations, carefully inked pictures of railway engines and mineshafts and factory looms, but he didn't have any train drivers or miners or factory hands because he can't draw people properly.

'I'll draw them in for you, Jamie,' I offered.

He turned down my generous offer. He didn't trust me. I wonder why!

He had lots of proper pictures too, cut out of real old illustrated Victorian papers, and samples of William Morris wallpaper, and photos of Victorian families standing up straight in their best clothes, and real Victorian coins carefully stuck in with Sellotape. Jamie's file was bulging already. My notebook was small and slim and there were still only a few pages of writing.

'You haven't done much yet, Charlie,' said Jamie, snatching it up and rifling through it.

'Give it *back*,' I said, trying to grab it.

'Why have you done it in this funny pencil writing? What's all this stuff? It's like a diary. "Well, I do not think Charlotte is a suitable name for a servant." What are you on about?' said Jamie, holding it just out of my reach.

'Don't you *dare* read it!' I said, and I gave him such a smack on the head he dropped my book instantly.

'Ooooow! What did you do that for?' he gasped, clutching his head.

'I warned you,' I said, clutching my book to my chest.

'You're mad! If you weren't a girl I'd sock you straight back,' said Jamie.

One side of his face was bright red and the shape of my hand. There were tears in his eyes. I felt a bit worried. I hadn't meant to hit him quite as hard as all that.

'You can try hitting me back but I wouldn't advise it,' I said. 'Just stop messing about with my private stuff, right?'

'It's just your Victorian project, for goodness' sake. And you're doing it all wrong, not a bit the way Miss Beckworth said.'

'I'm doing it *my* way,' I said.

'You'll get into trouble.'

'See if I care,' I said.

Miss Beckworth came into the classroom just then. She gave us all one quick glance – and then fixed her gaze on Jamie.

'What's the matter with you, James?' she said.

I held my breath. It looked as if I was in trouble right that minute. I expected Jamie to blab. He looked as if he were going to. But then he shrugged and shook his head. 'Nothing's the matter, Miss Beckworth,' he said.

I was amazed. And even more astonished when Miss Beckworth didn't pursue it. She just raised her eyebrows as if to say 'You can't kid me,' but then she sat down at her desk and started the lesson.

Jamie started working right away, one cheek still scarlet. I watched him for a while. I struggled with myself. Then I leant towards him. He flinched, as if he was scared I might slap him again.

'Why didn't you say I slapped you?' I whispered.

Jamie blinked at me nervously. 'I'm not a sneaky tell-tale,' he said.

'Well. Thanks,' I mumbled.

He didn't say anything back but his other cheek went red too.

So perhaps Jamie isn't one hundred per cent revolting and disgusting and infuriating. Just ninety-nine per cent. But as if I'd ever sit chewing my nails waiting for his phone call!

Nobody rang. Not a single soul required the services of the strong reliable schoolgirl.

'Why don't you ring him?' said Jo, still dopily deluded.

But the next day Miss Pease from downstairs waylaid her as she was stumbling back from her morning shift at the supermarket.

'Yes, Miss Pease wanted a little word about you, Charlie,' said Jo, hands on her hips.

'If she's nagging on about my music again she's nuts. I keep it turned down so soft I can barely hear it myself. She must have ears like Dumbo's,' I said, munching toast.

Jo snatched half of it from my plate. 'Here, spare a crumb for your poor hardworking mother,' she said. 'I'm starving.'

'So am I. You make your own. I've got to go to school.'

'Yes, well, you can wait a minute. Miss Pease says you've been soliciting.'

'I've been *what*?' I said.

'Well, that's the word she used,' said Jo. She was trying to sound stern, but she looked as if she might giggle any minute. 'Yes, that's what she said. "I really must bring this to your attention, Josephine. Charlotte has been soliciting."' Jo's voice wobbled.

I chuckled tentatively. It was a mistake.

'No, it's not funny, Charlie. What have you been playing at, posting all these little letters in people's flats offering to do work?'

'I was wanting to help out.'

'Oh, Charlie. You are a nutter. Miss Pease is right for once in her long and boring life. You can't advertise yourself like that, especially when there are such loonies around. Some weird guy might have read about this little schoolgirl wanting work and got some terrible ideas.'

'I'm not little, I'm big. And strong. But I take your point. Still, you don't have to fuss. No-one's phoned. Not a single sausage, and after all that money I spent on photocopying. It's daft. The whole idea was to *make* a bit of money.'

'Don't worry. That's my job. And anyway, it has worked in a way. Miss Pease says she's got a job for you.'

'Really?' I tried to feel pleased, but Miss Pease is such a pain. She's the sort of old lady who pats you on the head like a puppydog and relentlessly asks you how old you are, as if you might have aged five years since the last time you told her a week ago. Still, work is work.

Only this work was worse than most. You'll never guess what she wanted me to do. *Read* to her.

I don't really like reading aloud at the best of times. I don't like hearing my voice go all silly and showing-off. And that's when I can pick and choose my own book. Miss Pease wanted me to read her library book, one of those large big-print books that make your arms ache when you hold them up. My arms ached, my back ached, my head ached, my throat ached, my entire body was in ache overdrive after I read to Miss Pease for a whole hour.

It was this terrible stupid story about some dippy woman who kept being pursued in the desert by this total nutcase in a striped nightie. Well, that's what he was wearing on the book jacket. Instead of telling him to get lost sharpish the heroine simpered and swooned into the sand. I kid you not. And Miss Pease obviously adored this utter rubbish. She sat back literally licking her chops. Mind you, that might have been because of all the Cadbury's Milk Tray she  was eating. She got through a good half of the box.

'Of course I'd offer you one, Charlie dear, but you can't really read with your mouth full, can you?' she said.

'I can try,' I said hopefully.

She thought I was joking. And *I* thought she was joking when she handed over my wages for the reading session.

'Here you are, dear,' she said, fumbling in her purse. She handed me a ten-pence piece.

I stared at it. Had she mistaken it for a pound coin? Even so, what a totally mingy rate of pay!

'Pop it in your money box, dear,' said Miss Pease. 'And come back and read to me tomorrow.'

Not flipping likely! I was dead depressed, and annoyed when Jo just laughed and found it funny. But she was in a good mood because she'd got herself *another* job, cleaning this big posh house three days a week from ten to twelve.

'*Three* jobs!' she said, and she sent out for pizza with three extra toppings to celebrate.

'You'll exhaust yourself,' I said. 'What with getting up at five and doing the supermarket and then looking after the silly little sprog in the afternoons.'

'I'll be OK. And this new job's a doddle. The house is big, but they keep it very tidy. She's ever so worried about the idea of employing another woman to do her dirty work. I bet she runs round with the vacuum before I get there.'

'Where is it?' I asked, my mouth drooling cheese fronds.

'Oxford Terrace,' said Jo.

I stared at her, so shocked that my half of the pizza slipped out of my fingers onto the floor. I didn't care. I wasn't hungry any more.

FOOD

Oh, how I long for Mother's cooking. One of her
meaty stews, bubbling with
barley beans and carrots.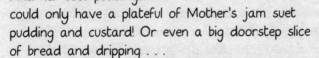
Or rabbit pie. Mother has
such a light touch when it
comes to making pastry.
Her fruit lattice pies are
famous all over the village.
And her suet puddings. If I
could only have a plateful of Mother's jam suet
pudding and custard! Or even a big doorstep slice
of bread and dripping . . .

I have to slice up the bread so thin here I slice
my fingers too, and Louisa won't eat her crusts
even then. The baby likes his bread pounded into
mush with warm milk. Mother would never dream
of pampering us so. We always ate what we
were given and chewed it cheerily. Well, mostly. But
Louisa always plays around with her food and
cries and complains something chronic, and Victor is
extremely pernickety for a boy, fuss fuss fussing if
he swallows a little lump in his custard. Sometimes
it's all I can do not to grab their plates and eat it

up for them because I'm so hungry. I have to manage on nursery food too, no meat at all during the week, and just one slice off the roast on Sundays. I am allowed one egg a week too, but it's a pale watery thing compared with the deep gold yolks laid by our hens at home.

I have to make do with this niminy-piminy fare with the merest scrape of butter. The only food that is plentiful is milk pudding. I shall start mooing before long.

'We don't want you to fall ill with too rich a diet,' says the Mistress, as if servants have different stomachs from posh folk.

Mrs Angel the cook and Eliza the maid are supposed to survive on this frugal diet too, but they eat their meals down in the kitchen and Mrs Angel is adept at keeping back the choicest portions for their own plates before Eliza serves the Master and Mistress in the dining room. I have my meals in the nursery so I miss out on these perks. Mrs Angel and Eliza treat me like one of the children anyway. They whisper and have secrets and laugh unkindly at the things I say. They are excessively tiresome. They are the childish pair. I do my best to ignore them, but then Mrs Angel calls me hoity toity and Eliza pulls my hair so that it tumbles down out of my cap. It is hard to bear sometimes. At home I was always a favourite. At school I was definitely Miss Worthbeck's pet. All the children loved me. Even the boys. Yes, even that great lummox Edward James. But now I am openly despised and it makes my heart sore. At night I cry into my pillowcase, the sheets pulled right over my head so the children will not hear me.

Victor sees my red eyes in the morning and says that I have been blubbing.

'Nonsense,' I say firmly. 'I have a slight cold, that is all.'

Perhaps that was tempting fate. Now the whole household has gone down with colds, even little baby Freddie. Mrs Angel has taken to her bed and Eliza is trying to take charge of the kitchen, but with very bad grace. The Mistress says her ailing children must have calves' foot jelly served to them at every meal. I ask Eliza to prepare it but she utterly refuses, saying she has her work cut out as it is and she cannot abide messing around with lumps of messy meat.

So I have to make the jelly. The whole kitchen reeks and the walls glisten as the calves' feet boil and boil and boil, and I skim and skim and skim, and then when I go to strain the liquid through the jelly bag my hands slip and . . . disaster! By the time I have run out to the butcher's for six more calves' feet and started the whole business in motion all over again I am in such savage spirits that I would cheer if a whole herd of calves stampeded through the house and trampled everyone within it with their poor feet.

TOYS AND BOOKS

I was so scared! Jo could be cleaning Jamie Edwards's house. I could just imagine Jamie lounging on a velvet chaise-longue in his posh William Morris-papered parlour, snapping his fingers imperiously at Jo.

'Hey, you! Cleaning lady! Get me another cushion,' he'd command. 'I've spilt crumbs all over the carpet so get cracking with the hoover. And don't sigh like that or I'll dock your wages.'

I could see it as clear as anything. Poor Jo would have to wash Jamie's clothes and tidy Jamie's bed and dust all Jamie's possessions. Maybe Jamie had a brace of younger brothers just as bratty as him, and she'd have to wash their clothes and tidy their beds and dust their toys. If he had a baby brother she'd maybe even have to wash and tidy and dust *him* down.

'It's not your Jamie Edwards's house,' said Jo. 'This is the Rosen family, Mr

62

and Mrs, with two teenage daughters.'

I practically passed out with relief.

'Are you disappointed?' said Jo. 'Did you hope I'd get to go in your Jamie's bedroom, eh, to tell you all about the posters on his wall and whether he still has a teddy on his bed and maybe even have a sneaky peek in his diary to see if he ever writes anything about you?'

'He's not *my* Jamie!' I shrieked. 'You are so nuts, Jo. I keep telling you, I can't stick him.'

Jo wasn't the only one who teased me about terrible Jamie Edwards. Lisa and Angela had started up this stupid game too. I was starting to get seriously annoyed with them. I didn't know what had got into them this year at school. Last year we were the three leaders of nearly all the girls and we had this special club badge with GAB on it, short for 'Girls Are Best', and we all called each other Gabby and we had this cheerleader chant I made up: 'Girls are best, Never mind the rest, Boys are a pest, So *Girls are best!*'

Some of the other girls got a bit fed up and drifted away but Lisa and Angela and I kept up our special girls' gang all the time, and the three of us always went yuck and pulled a face whenever any of the boys spoke to us. I wanted to extend the rules to cover men too, but Lisa said that was daft because her dad was a man and she loved him better than anyone else in the whole world, and Angela was equally awkward and got this immense crush on this pop star and squealed whenever she saw him on

63

the telly and she stuck hundreds of pictures of him all over her bedroom walls and kissed every one of them goodnight when she went to bed and she did inky designs of his name entwined with hers all over her school books and her ruler and her bag and even on the sleeve of her jacket, though her mum got very narked about that.

Lisa and I thought Angela had gone incredibly crackers because this guy she likes is *pathetic*. Angela agrees with us now, and she's torn down all his pictures and crossed out his name and she's got a new jacket – but she's in love with another pop group now, *all* of them, and she's forever striking up these boring boring boring conversations about what she'd do if she could only get to meet them.

I knew that if only I'd been able to sit next to Angela at school as I'd planned then I'd have been able to be a good influence on her and keep her under control. She was starting to get on my nerves so much I was wondering about whittling my best friends down to one. But then Lisa fell in love too. And that was worse. Because she started to go crazy over David Wood – and he's certainly not a famous star in a band, he's just this ultra-boring boy in our class at school.

'He's not ultra-boring!' Lisa squeaked. 'He's dead cool. I love the way he does his hair. And his eyes. And he looks really old for his age, doesn't he, because he's so tall.'

'He might look old but he acts like a

64

toddler,' I said, disgusted. 'Didn't you see him in the canteen throwing his lunch around?'

'That was just his bit of fun,' said Lisa. 'One of his chips landed right in my lap!'

'Oh wow! How could you contain your excitement,' I said, dead sarcastic.

'She ate it too!' said Angela. 'After he'd drooled all over it.'

'I wouldn't mind if he drooled all over *me,*' said Lisa.

'Oh shut *up,*' I said. 'Honestly. I think you had a lobotomy in the summer holiday.'

'A lobby-what?' said Lisa.

'It's an operation they perform on your brain,' I said. 'Don't you know anything?'

'I know one thing, Charlie Enright. You're getting a right pain, always showing off and looking down your nose at other people. You're getting just like Jamie Edwards.'

'Yeah, maybe it's rubbing off on her because they sit together,' said Angela, giggling in this particularly irritating way. 'Hey, Lisa – Charlie and Jamie, what a pair, eh?'

'They're always yacking away together, certainly. Miss Beckworth had to tell them off the other day, they were getting so carried away,' said Lisa, giving Angela a nudge.

'You're the one who's in danger of getting carried away – in a body bag,' I said, giving them both a simultaneous example of *my* sort of nudge. I have very very sharp elbows. 'I hardly *ever* speak to Jamie

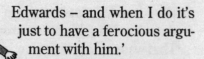

Edwards – and when I do it's just to have a ferocious argument with him.'

However, I needed to speak to Jamie in a dead-casual, almost-friendly way to find out exactly where he lived in Oxford Terrace. He knew what Jo looked like. We'd both been going to this school since we were practically babies. For years and years our mums had delivered us or collected us. I had noticed that Jamie's mum was plump and beady-eyed like him, with lots of hair and jazzy jumpers and coloured tights and bright boots, none of them matching. He had probably noticed that Jo was much younger than the other mums, and dyed her hair to match mine and wore high heels to make her just a tiny bit taller.

It's awfully hard to strike up a dead-casual, almost-friendly conversation with someone you can't stick. We're barely allowed to breathe in Miss Beckworth's classes anyway, let alone converse. But at playtime I took ages putting away my books and let Lisa and Angela go off by themselves. Jamie always took his time too, not at all keen to go out into the playground. He's not the outdoor type. He's hopeless at football and he can't even run properly, his arms and legs go every which way. He isn't bullied by the other boys because he can be quite quick and cutting with what he says, but he's not exactly number one popular person with his peers. (Not like *some* people I could mention if I wanted to be disgustingly boastful.)

He generally slopes off into a corner by himself and reads a book. I watched him take one out of his satchel. It was covered in the Victorian wrapping paper so you couldn't see the title.

'What's that you're reading then, Jamie?' I asked.

He looked at me suspiciously. 'Why?'

'I just want to know, for goodness' sake,' I said.

'With you it's usually for badness' sake,' said Jamie.

'Let's have a look, then,' I said, reaching for it.

He hesitated, holding it away from me. 'Are you going to hit me again if I don't let you?' he said.

'That was different. That was *my* book. So what's yours? Why have you got it all wrapped up like that? Hey, it's a dirty book, that's it, isn't it! Shock, scandal, swotty old Jamie's reading a rude book. And you didn't want anyone to see you're reading it. What is it, eh? Show me!'

'Get off!' said Jamie, trying to push me away, but he was still wary of me. I snatched his book easily and opened it.

'"Esther Waters",' I read, flicking through the pages. 'Oooh! What a swizzle. It's just some boring boring boring old Victorian book. Typical you, Jamie Edwards. You're just doing some extra swotting up for your project, aren't you?'

'The Victorians thought it was a rude book,' said Jamie. 'They were ever so shocked when it came out.'

'Well, they were shocked by anything. They were

so stupid they even covered up their piano legs! If a woman raised her skirt a few inches above her ankles the chaps practically fainted dead away,' I said scornfully. 'So what does this Esther Waters get up to,  Jamie? Is she so dead brazen she flashes her kneecaps?'

'Oh, ha ha,' said Jamie, sighing.

I saw he had his bookmark more than halfway through.

'Gosh, have you read all that? It looks *terribly* dull and difficult. You're mad,' I said.

'It's a good story actually,' said Jamie. 'It's about this girl Esther—'

'No!'

'—and she's a servant and—'

'She's a servant?' I said, stopping messing about.

'Yes, and she goes to this big place in the country and this footman chats her up and she doesn't really want to go out with him but he forces her and she ends up having a baby and she doesn't know what to do because she's young and she's not married and she's lost her job . . . Why are you staring at me like that?' said Jamie. 'What is it?'

'Nothing. It just doesn't sound quite as boring as I thought. Maybe I'll borrow it after you, OK?'

I mostly stuck to reading horror stories, the spookier and scarier the better, but I wanted to find out more about this Esther.

'What happens to her? Does she keep her baby?

Does she get a job? She doesn't get married at the end, does she?'

'I haven't got that far yet. OK, you can borrow it after me. Or some of my other books if you want. I've got a whole lot of Victorian ones sorted out because of my project.'

'Oh, Jamie, you would!' I said. Then I suddenly realized this was my golden opportunity. 'So, I might come round to your famous Victorian house sometime and see your books. What number Oxford Terrace, eh?'

'Number sixty-two,' said Jamie.

I felt my stomach squeeze. Number 62. Jo's Rosen family lived at Number 58, next door but one to Jamie. What if he saw her going into their house? What if Jamie's mum nipped along the road to have a cup of coffee with Mrs Rosen when Jo was dashing around with a duster? What if Jamie's mum thought Jo looked dead handy with a hoover and offered her a job? I was proud that she was working so hard but I couldn't *stand* the idea of her cleaning all Jamie's junk.

'Has your mum got her own cleaning lady?' I blurted out before I could stop myself.

Jamie blinked at me, baffled. 'What? Why? Are you scared you'll get all dusty if you come round to my house?' he said.

'Does your mum do her own dusting?' I persisted.

'No. Mum's hopeless at any sort of housework. We did have a cleaning lady once but then she got ill and—'

'You're not looking for another one, are you?' I asked, horrified.

'My dad does the housework now. The hoovering and that. Mum might do the bathroom, and I'm supposed to do some stuff, me and my brother, only we skive off mostly. *Why?*'

I shrugged elaborately. 'I – I've got interested in the whole idea of housework and stuff because of my servant project,' I said.

Angela and Lisa put their heads round the classroom door.

'Come *on*, Charlie. Playtime's nearly over. What are you doing?' said Angela.

'Of course, we don't want to interrupt anything if you and Jamie are *busy*,' said Lisa, giggling.

'I'm *coming*,' I said, charging over to them.

 But then that idiotic Jamie put his great big foot in it. 'So, you're coming round to my house after school tonight, right?' he said, in front of Lisa and Angela. Their mouths dropped open. Mine did too.

'Wrong!' I said, and rushed off.

Lisa and Angela rushed too.

'We were just kidding you before. But you really have got a thing going with Jamie, haven't you?' said Angela.

'You're going round to his *house*!' said Lisa. 'Oh, I do wish Dave would ask me round to *his* house.'

'I'm not *going* round to Jamie Edwards's house,' I insisted. 'He was just going on about these boring

boring boring Victorian books and he seemed to think I was mad enough to want to look at them, that's all.' My heart was thumping a bit as I said it. I knew I was kind of twisting the truth. But I had to stop Lisa and Angela getting the wrong idea once and for all.

So all that day I sent them notes under the quivering Beckworth nose as often as I dared, with silly caricatures of Jamie and rude little rhymes about him. Jamie saw his name and must have thought I was writing a note to him. He peered over my arm and read it. I'd just written a *very* rude bit about him. (Sorry: far too rude to be repeated where adults like Miss Beckworth might whip this book out of your hands at any minute!) Jamie read the very rude bit. He blinked. He didn't look baffled this time. He looked upset.

Still, it was his own fault, wasn't it? He shouldn't have been nosy enough to read my private note. I passed it to Angela and she cracked up with silent laughter and then she passed it on to Lisa and she read it and snorted out loud and had to protest to Miss Beckworth that she had a horrible cold and couldn't help it. Lisa and Angela and I all fell about helplessly when we came out of school.

I certainly didn't go round to Jamie's house after school. Lisa and I went round to Angela's house first because her big brother had just got some dead flash roller blades for his birthday and we were hoping we'd get to her home from our school a good

71

half-hour before he got back from *his* school, so we could all maybe have a sneaky go on his blades. But he'd got wise to Angela's wily ways and installed a brand-new padlock on his bedroom cupboard. We found his old skateboard stacked in a corner but we weren't really into skateboarding any more, and anyway, one of the wheels was all wobbly.

Angela's mum was doing a day shift at the hospital so she couldn't fix us anything exciting to eat so we all went round to Lisa's instead. That was far more promising, because Lisa's mum was being a hostess for a jewellery party that evening and so she was making all these fiddly little vol-au-vents and tarts. She let us sample them while she got busy icing a cake. Lisa wanted us to go straight up to her bedroom, but I hung around her mum for a bit, watching how she did the icing with this natty little squeezy bag.

'I always wondered how people wrote those little messages,' I said. 'Is it difficult?'

'No, pet, it's easy as anything,' said Lisa's mum, and when she had finished she let me practise icing these cookies she'd baked. I iced my name and then Lisa's and then Angela's. That was dead crafty, because we got to eat them!

I asked Lisa's mum how she made the cake and she thought I was angling for a slice of that too.

'Sorry, pet. I'm saving it for the ladies at my party. Hey, maybe your mother would like to come?'

72

She hesitated. 'I mean, just for the chit-chat at the party. I know she's not really in a position to buy any jewellery right this moment.'

'She goes to bed really early now. Because she has to get up at five for this new job,' I said.

Lisa's mum's smooth face went into a crease of pain.

'Oh my goodness. She's being so *brave*,' she said, as if Jo went and wrestled with a pit of poisonous snakes instead of one unwieldy industrial cleaner.

'But I really would like to know how to make a sponge cake like that. We don't make cakes at home,' I said.

'Well, it's so simple. And really not very expensive. Tell your mother you just need to put the butter and the sugar and the flour in the blender and—'

'No, we haven't got a blender.'

Lisa's mum stared as if I'd said we hadn't got a *kitchen*.

'Oh. Well. I suppose you could mix it all by hand. I know!' She went to her shelf of cookery books beside the spice rack and pulled out an old fat book; the pages had gone a little yellow. She flicked through it.

'Aha! This was *my* mother's cookery book. She certainly didn't have a blender. Yes, there's a whole section on cake-making. Do you think your mother would like to borrow it?'

'It's not for Jo, it's for me. I'd *love* to borrow it,' I said eagerly. 'I want to suss out how to make cakes. Proper ones, not the packet sort.'

'Well, good for you. I wish my Lisa would get interested in cookery. You're a strange girl, Charlie. You've always seemed such a tomboy. I never thought you'd get keen on cake-making. Still, you're all getting older. It's only natural you're changing.'

'I'm not changing,' I said quickly.

'What's that saying? "Too old for toys but too young for boys." Though my Lisa has certainly started on boys already. It's Dave this and Dave that until we're sick of the sound of him! Which boy do you like, Charlie?'

'None of them,' I said firmly.

'Give it another six months,' said Lisa's mum, smiling at me.

I had to stay polite because she'd just lent me the cookery book but when I got home to Jo I moaned like anything.

'She's treating me like I'm retarded or something,' I said. 'Like I still play with my Barbie dolls.'

'What's wrong with Barbie dolls?' said Jo.

She used to buy me lots of Barbies with all their different outfits and we'd dress them up and drive them round in their Cadillac and take them to the disco and make them bop up and down on their tiny high heels. I think Jo liked playing Barbie games just as much as I did. If not more. I wanted to chuck all mine out ages ago but she wouldn't let me.

'Store them in a drawer and keep them for *your* daughter,' she said.

74

So they're stored. I took off all their glitzy little outfits and laid them on their backs in my underwear drawer and covered them with bits of old pillow case, playing one last ritual game with them. Mortuaries.

Jo got totally unnerved when she opened the drawer looking for spare socks.

'Have you come to view the corpses?' I said.

'You are a seriously weird child.'

'It's coming from a single-parent family,' I said. 'I'm seriously deprived. It's no wonder I'm weird.'

I was only joking of course. I *like* being a select family of two. Jo and me. And that's the way it's always going to be.

TOYS AND BOOKS

I cannot believe the toys the children have here!
Victor has a dappled rocking horse as big as the
old pony in the field behind our cottage at home.
It's such a splendid creature, with a curly mane
and a long tail of real horse's hair, a red saddle
and reins and great green rockers. Louisa begs and
begs Victor to let her take a turn but he will
rarely agree. Once when the children were
downstairs with the Mistress I stood staring
at the rocking horse. Before I knew what I
was doing I had hitched my skirts above
my knees and clambered into the
saddle. I fingered the curly mane and
stroked the smooth shining wood,
and then I dared lean forward and
rock once, twice, three times. The
rockers creaked and I did not dare
persist in case they could hear me down
below.

Louisa's china doll seemed to watch with her
blue glass eyes. Her painted red lips were open as
if she might tell. But I must not be fanciful. She is
only a doll. But a beautiful doll all the same, with

76

golden ringlets and three sets of fine clothes. She
even has little lace mittens for her tiny china
fingers, imagine! I have had to help Louisa on and
off with those clothes, stripping the doll right down
to her white silk drawers. She has three petticoats,
two silk and one flannel, and white cotton stock—
ings and little soft kid shoes, three pairs,
in black and grey and pink for
parties. Three pairs of shoes
for a doll that cannot
walk. Rose and Jessie
and I have never had soft
shoes. We'd run around barefoot
in the summer and plod in our old boots
throughout the winter. How Rose and Jessie would
love Louisa's dolls, and the dolls' house with all the
furniture — little chairs and tables, a four-poster
bed no less, and even a miniature mop and mangle
in the scullery!

We had our own halfpenny dolls at home,
one each in our Christmas stockings, and
we'd sew them little dresses and make
them a home in an old
wooden crate, the
same crate that was
once our Frank's boat
and carriage. Sometimes I
gave baby Ada—May a
ride in that old crate and
she crowed with delight . . .

Oh, how I miss her. How I miss Rose

and Jessie. I even miss Frank. I miss dear Mother
most of all. I write to her once a week,
unburdening my heart. I hope Rose reads my letters
properly to Mother. She can read well enough when
she wants, but she hurries so over the words.
Mother was kept at home as a child to mind her
own young brothers and sisters so she never
learnt to read. She used to marvel after I went to
the village school and learnt to spell out words.

Miss Worthbeck let me read aloud to the
children on Friday afternoons from wonderful
story books, *Alice* and *The Water Babies* and some
of Mr Dickens's books. I do not wish to boast but
she once said I had Shining Intelligence.

My Shining Intelligence is tarnishing rapidly now I
am a nursery maid.

FAMILY

It was Grandma and Grandpa's Pearl Wedding anniversary in a couple of weeks.

'We're not having a party,' said Grandma. 'That's not our way.' She spoke as if parties were incredibly vulgar, on a par with naked mud wrestling in pig sties. 'We thought we'd like to celebrate the occasion with a special Sunday lunch.' She paused. 'Just for the family.'

She meant Jo and me. Once she was off the phone we moaned and groaned, trying to think up wild excuses to get out of it. We don't like going to Grandma and Grandpa's at the best of times.

'And this will be the worst,' said Jo. 'They'll talk about their wedding and their anniversaries, all thirty of them. Grandma will fiddle with her wedding and engagement and eternity rings. She might *even* get out their wedding album. Oh help, she might even delve in the trunk upstairs and come out with this truly horrible yellowy-white lace veil and then her voice will go all shaky when she says she kept it specially for me to wear at my wedding. And then she'll stop and sigh because I didn't ever have a wedding. Watch out, Charlie. She'll be saving it for you now.'

'*I'm* not going to get married!' I insisted. 'I'm going to stay here with you. I look old for my age and you look young so by the time I'm grown up we'll just be like two sisters. I'll be earning too so it'll be easy-peasy, simple-pimple paying that old mortgage.'

'I wish!' said Jo.

We didn't have any spare cash for Pearl Wedding presents so we had to be inventive. Jo bought a half-price droopy pot plant and fed and watered it until it stood up straight and grew new glossy leaves. She bought some pearl-white ribbon and then tied thirty tiny bows all over it.

'There? Do you think it'll do?' she said, tying the very last bow.

'It looks lovely.'

'It's nowhere near as impressive as your cake.'

Yes, I'd made Grandma and Grandpa a proper cake! I used Lisa's mum's recipe book. I couldn't do a fruit cake because the ingredients were too expensive. I just did a sponge. Well, I did three sponges if you must know. I didn't quite get the hang of it the first time and failed to realize you had to mix it all like crazy until your arm practically falls off. There was just this surly sulky crust at the bottom of the tin when I took it out of the oven. The second go was better, but I was too eager, opening the oven door a couple of times to see how it was getting on.

It didn't rise properly and so I left it in longer and then it got a bit burnt. I cut off the burnt bits and made it into a trifle, but even so, I was starting to think I was squandering money instead of saving it. Jo said I should have one more go and *this* time it was third time lucky. My sponge was *perfect*.

Now I could get started on the best bit. I covered it with apricot glaze to stop any crumbs getting mixed up with the icing. Then I piped *Happy Aniversary* across the top of the icing and made little rosettes all the way round and studded it with tiny pearly balls. It took ages but I was so proud when I'd finished. Jo looked worried when I showed it off to her.

'What?'

'It's beautiful,' she said. 'They'll love it.'

Ha! They didn't love it. Or Jo's plant. Grandpa nodded and said, 'How delightful. Thank you so much. How thoughtful of you. But you really shouldn't have.'

That sounds OK down on paper. But my grandpa speaks in this slow serious voice with hardly any expression. He doesn't go *Wow!* or hug or kiss. If he ever touches me accidentally he wipes his hands on his hankie afterwards, as if I'm sticky.

Grandma uses enough expression for two. 'Oh, darlings, we weren't expecting *presents*. Especially in your current circumstances. Josephine, I've been very worried about your new job, you've hardly told me anything about it.'

'Look at the cake Charlie's made you. She did it all herself. It took her ages,' said Jo.

'Yes, it's *lovely*, dear. Yum yum. We'll all have a slice for tea.' But Grandma sighed. 'What a pity!'

'What?' I said.

'I can't wait to sample this cake,' said Jo quickly. She was sending signals with her eyebrows to Grandma. Grandma ignored them.

'It's such a shame you left out the "n", dear.'

I'd left out one of the 'n's in *Anniversary*. Even though I *knew* how to spell it. I couldn't stand it. I'd thought it really was perfect.

'As if that matters,' Jo said, furious with Grandma for pointing it out.

'Well, as a matter of fact, I *do* think spelling matters although I know they don't pay much attention to it in school nowadays,' said Grandma, putting my cake on her kitchen table. She took the pot plant to the sink.

'It doesn't need watering yet. I did it yesterday,' said Jo.

'I just want to perk it up a little,' said Grandma.

She should have watered Jo and me. We were visibly drooping. I can never work out if Grandma knows what she's doing. She's certainly an expert at chewing you up and spitting you out in tiny pieces. No wonder it took Jo months and months before she dared tell them she was going to have me.

Grandma and Grandpa still treat her like a schoolgirl in disgrace. Grandma kept on and on about her old job while she put the vegetables on to cook, prodding Jo as sharply as the potatoes. Jo lied a lot but she's not as good at it as me. Grandma didn't even shut up when we started eating.

'What do you *mean*, Josephine? What does this new supermarket job entail?' Grandma attacked her grapefruit, jabbing at it with a serrated spoon. 'You're being deliberately evasive. Are you sure you're not working as a cashier on the tills?'

Jo suddenly flung down her own spoon, going as red as the glacé cherries Grandma used for decoration. 'I am not a cashier,' she said. 'I am a cleaner at the supermarket. So now you know.'

Grandma sputtered like the hot fat cooking her roast beef. She gave Jo a roasting all the while we chewed on our meat. She told Jo it wasn't a suitable job when she'd been a manager for nearly a year, as if Jo had deliberately turned down umpteen other manager's jobs just to be contrary. She told Jo she was being an irresponsible mother going out early in the morning and leaving me, and that made me so mad I had to put in my two-pennyworth.

'I think *you're* being the irresponsible mother to Jo, telling her off and being so horrible when Jo's tried so hard to sort things out. I think she's wonderful to get up so early and trudge off like that. *I'm* OK, I'm still in my bed. Jo has to get up early every single morning except Sunday, and she should be having a lovely long lie-in today, but she couldn't, because we had to get the train and the

bus right over to your place to wish you a Happy Anniversary – *two* 'n's – only you're just mucking it all up.'

They were all staring at me. 'That's quite enough, young lady!' said Grandma.

'You're not my mother so you can't tell me off,' I said. 'Jo? Do you want me to shut up?'

'Yes!' said Jo. 'Come on, Charlie, we'd better go home.'

'Now don't be ridiculous. We haven't even started on pudding yet,' said Grandma.

'Why don't you all do a lot more chewing and a lot less yapping,' said Grandpa, calmly working his way through his second helping of roast beef.

So we sat still and no-one said anything. Jo and I left a lot on our plates. So did Grandma. But Grandpa didn't even leave a glisten of gravy.

I didn't think I'd be able to eat pudding. It was pineapple upside-down cake and my own stomach felt upside-down too. But I tried a tiny bit and it was actually good, so I ate a bit more, and then a bit more still, until I'd finished it all up.

Grandpa nodded in approval. He finished his last mouthful too.

'Now that you've all calmed down, perhaps we ought to discuss your financial situation, Josephine,' he said.

I wanted to tell him it was none of his business. But even I didn't quite dare cheek Grandpa.

Jo stammered a little as she told him that we were managing, and she'd sorted things out with the building society to give us a little leeway, and she didn't just have the one job, she had three, and she was still looking for another supervisory position all the time. She said it all as if he was giving her a formal interview. Grandpa nodded, occasionally easing the collar of his shirt where it rubbed his neck. He never wears casual clothes, not even at weekends. I couldn't remotely imagine him in something like a T-shirt. I can't even picture him in his under-wear. I don't think Grandpa has an ordinary body at all, he's just hard smooth plastic underneath like a Ken doll.

Grandma wanted to know all about the other cleaning jobs. She raised her eyebrows and looked pained when Jo told her about the Oxford Terrace job, but she actually leant forward and looked interested when she heard about Robin, the little boy Jo picks up from school.

'So what's his father like?' said Grandma, suddenly all ears. I could actually see them getting pink underneath her neat grey curls.

I sighed and flopped back in my chair. This was so *typical* Grandma. She can't even get it into her head that Jo *likes* being a single mum and isn't remotely interested in meeting any men. Grandma used to keep trying to introduce Jo to all these creeps, and she nagged her to join a Singles club and she even once advertised Jo in a Lonely Hearts column. She did, I kid you not. She thinks if she can only get Jo married off then she won't have to be ashamed of us any more.

I waggled my eyebrows at Jo, expecting her to wink back. But she wasn't looking at me. She wasn't looking at anyone. She was staring at the shiny yellow pudding on her plate as if Robin's father was reflected there.

'He's very nice,' she said. Her tone was brisk – but she blushed.

I stared at her. Grandma was staring too.

'Very nice?' said Grandma impatiently. 'What *sort* of very nice? What job does he do? What does he look like? What's happened to the boy's mother?'

'He's very nice – what more can I say?' said Jo. 'He's something in the Civil Service.'

'Which grade?' said Grandma.

'As if I know!'

'Is he good looking?'

'I suppose so. In a kind of lean, lost sort of way,' said Jo.

'Mmm!' said Grandma. 'And is he a widower?'

'No. His wife left him. She had custody of Robin at first, but he didn't get on with the boyfriend, so now he's back with his dad.'

'And Dad doesn't have a girlfriend?'

'No. Well. He could have. But he hasn't mentioned one,' said Jo.

'She's just his cleaner,' I said crossly. 'She doesn't have anything to do with him, do you, Jo?'

'No. That's right. Yes,' said Jo, sounding muddled.

I frowned at her. What was she on about? And why did she have that stupid little smile on her face? I suddenly got terribly anxious. What was going on?

Jo hadn't ever said anything about this man to me. Well. She'd said he was nice. Very nice. But that's such a limp nothing sort of comment that I didn't even notice it at the time.

I didn't have a clue what he was really like. I'd never met him. I had met Robin. It was easier for Jo to bring him round to our place after she'd met him from school.

'It's so I can be here for you too, Charlie. We can all have a snack together,' said Jo. 'Then I can take him home and do a spot of cleaning before his dad gets back.'

I wasn't at all keen on this idea, but I couldn't really object much to Robin. He wasn't like an ordinary boy of five at all. He was very little, with a long thick fringe and huge dark eyes in a white face. He gnawed nervously at his bottom lip all the time, and he trembled for the first few visits. He was like one of those small furry nocturnal creatures you see in the zoo, hunched at the bottom of their cage.

Robin

He certainly didn't run amok, messing up all my things. He sat where he was put, picking anxiously at the scabs on his bony bare knees, going nibble nibble nibble at his lips. Jo brought him books and he looked at them obediently. Jo found him paper and crayons and he drew neat square houses with a mummy on one side and a daddy on the other and a very tiny Robin in the middle, under the house. He wasn't any good at perspective so it looked as if the house was falling on him, about to 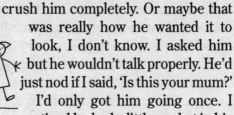 crush him completely. Or maybe that was really how he wanted it to look, I don't know. I asked him but he wouldn't talk properly. He'd just nod if I said, 'Is this your mum?' I'd only got him going once. I noticed he had a little pocket in his school sweatshirt that he patted every now and then. I thought he was checking up on his handkerchief. Robin was the sort of little boy who always breathes heavily and has a runny nose. He kept sniffling one afternoon so I told him rather sharply to use his handkerchief.

He looked stricken. He didn't move.

'Your hankie! Your nose is running. Yuck!' I said.

He shrivelled away from me, practically going inside the neck of his sweatshirt.

'Stop nagging him, Charlie. Here, we've got some tissues somewhere,' said Jo.

'But look, he's got his hankie with him,' I said, putting my hand in his pocket and pulling something out.

It wasn't a hankie. It was a little fluffy toy.

'That's mine! Give him back!' said Robin, and he darted forward, grabbing.

'Hey, OK! Don't get in such a flap. Here's your

88

little toy. What is it?' I said, peering.

Robin held it tight against his chest.

'Is he shy, your little animal?' I said. 'Oh
yes, he is, isn't he? Sorry. Didn't mean to
frighten him. He's looking at me with one
big beady eye. I think he really wants to
make friends. Are you going to get
him to say hello to me, Robin?'

Robin didn't seem sure. He fidgeted, not meeting
my eyes – but he seemed almost to be joining in the
game.

'Hello, little shy animal,' I said into Robin's
clasped hands.

'He's not an animal,' said Robin. 'He's a bird. He's
Birdie.'

Birdie edged his beak into the air so that I could
see.

'Oh, so he is! Hello, Birdie. Can you fly?' I said.

Robin nodded, and made Birdie nod too.

'I don't believe you,' I said.

'He can!' said Robin, and Birdie's beak went up
and down.

'No. I'm sure he can't possibly fly,' I said.

'Yes, he can, I'll show you,' said Robin, and
he unclenched his fist so that Birdie's woollen
wings flapped free. Robin stood up and skipped
round the kitchen, making his arm swoop up and
down. Birdie flew along with him. He had
two black bead eyes, a yellow beak, and
big brown wings, carefully scalloped at the
edge. He wore a bright-red knitted waistcoat.

Birdie

89

'I get it! Birdie's a Robin, like you,' I said.

Robin nodded happily, and Birdie flew faster.

'Did your mum make him for you?' I said without thinking.

Robin stopped. Birdie lost height rapidly and landed. Jo frowned at me from across the kitchen. Robin went and sat on a chair without saying another word. I didn't know whether his mum had made Birdie or not.

'I'm sorry, Robin,' I muttered.

I wondered what it would feel like if your mum didn't really want you. I knew what it felt like not to have a dad, but then that was OK. I didn't want one. Certainly not one like mine. When I was really little, younger than Robin, Jo used to tell me all these fairy tales about a lovely daddy who was so sad he couldn't see me, but I soon twigged she wasn't telling the truth. I asked her straight and so she told me straight. My dad was Jo's first boyfriend. She loved him like crazy but he was never so keen on her. Then when she found out she was going to have me she told him and he didn't want to know. 'That's your problem,' he said. I've been Jo's 'problem' ever since but we manage just fine.

Robin doesn't look like he's managing very well, even if he's still got this very nice dad. If he *is* very nice.

I don't like the sound of him.

FAMILY

It is our Jessie's birthday today. She is five years old, quite the little lady. I have been fretting over what to send her for a birthday present. Louisa has so many discarded toys in her trunk. There's a little china tea—set our Jessie would adore. Louisa packed it away so carelessly all the little teacups fell out of their cardboard setting and the lid of the sugar pot seems to be lost for ever.

'I don't care about that old tea—set, not now I have my new willow—pattern set,' said Louisa.

I very nearly asked her if I could have it for my little sister. Louisa might have said yes, but I didn't think the Mistress would like it. There are many many many things the Mistress doesn't like!

I did not risk taking so much as one tiny teacup for Jessie's present. I cut up one of my old black stockings that had worn away to holes and sat up sewing half the night, turning it into a little toy monkey like the one that sits on the organ—grinder's shoulder. I wanted to give him a little jacket and cap too, so I cut a square out of my red flannel petticoat. It will not show, after all. The monkey looked splendid in his fine red clothes. My eyes were red too the next day from sewing by candlelight and I was desperately tired, but I did not care for once. I wrapped the monkey in a piece of last week's newspaper and tied it with string and inked the address really large and clear upon the front and posted it off in plenty of time.

I felt happy for the first time since I have been working here. But now I feel sad, because I cannot see Jessie opening her present. I cannot give her a birthday kiss. I am so scared Jessie might forget all about me as I can only go home one day a year, on Mothering Sunday. Baby Ada-May will think me a total stranger. It makes my heart break.

The Mistress came into the nursery unexpectedly and found me weeping with my head in the wardrobe.

'Whatever is the matter, Charlotte?' she said. 'You are not ill, are you?'

'No, Madam.'

'Then why are you crying? Make haste with Miss Louisa's dress, or the child will get a chill.'

'Yes, Madam. Sorry, Madam. I'm just sad because I miss my family so.'

'You are part of this family now,' said the Mistress.

She said it as if she were granting me an immense

privilege. But I do not care for this family. How can I be part of it when I can never answer back or say what I really think? How can I feel really close to these children when I have to call them Miss and Master? I have to look after them all the time but there is no—one to look after me.

COURTSHIP

'I look such a mess,' Jo wailed.

'You look fine,' I said. Though she didn't. She had two spots and her hair needed washing and her sweater had shrunk and her leggings were all baggy at the knee.

'I'm going to have to change,' said Jo, diving into the bedroom. 'Keep an eye on Robin for me.'

I frowned after her. I went and fetched a drawing pad and felt tip pens. I put them in front of Robin on the kitchen table.

'Right. You can do a drawing with my own personal set of super felt tip pens – so long as you promise not to press too hard on the points, OK?'

'OK,' said Robin eagerly, because I didn't often let him borrow them. He was used to making do with his own little-boy wax crayons.

He picked up the red, ready to draw his usual neat square house.

'Don't draw any of that boring old house and mummy and daddy stuff. Why don't you pretend

Birdie's grown ginormous and you get on his back and you both fly away to a Magic Land where anything can happen. Draw that.'

Robin blinked at me doubtfully.

'Go on,' I said, giving him a little nudge. 'I'm just going to go and have a talk with my mother, OK? Do not disturb us unless it's a dire emergency like you've been seized with an uncontrollable desire to stick two felt tips simultaneously into your eyes and you need immediate medical attention.'

Robin nibbled his lip, glancing nervously at the tin of felt tips as if they might spontaneously attack him.

I sighed and marched into the bedroom. Jo had pulled off her old cleaning clothes and was standing in her underwear, making faces at her clothes in the wardrobe.

'Yuck,' she said. 'They're all old and grotty and rubbish.' She scratched her head. 'Double yuck. So am I. I've *got* to wash my hair. I was going to do it yesterday but I was so blooming tired and then there wasn't time to do more than splash my face this morning. Oh God, I think I'll climb into the washing machine at the Rosens' tomorrow morning and give myself a good soaping . . .' She went burbling on like this, to herself rather than me, as she made for the bathroom in her knickers, remembered Robin, went back for her tatty old dressing gown, and then stripped off and stepped into the bath. 'Do you think we'll ever have enough spare cash to have a shower installed?' she shouted over the roaring taps. 'Pass us that Snoopy mug, Charlie

– and the shampoo. What is it, eh? 'Cause I'm in a tearing hurry.'

'Why are you fussing about what you look like?' I said, sitting on the loo.

'What?' Jo said, tipping water over her head.

'Why are you washing your hair *now*?'

'Oh, for goodness' sake. My hair's all lank and disgusting, that's why,' said Jo, exasperated. She lathered shampoo in and then wiped the bathroom mirror clear of steam and looked at herself. '*Look* at me. Spots all over the place. And huge great bags under my eyes. It's not fair. I thought all this hard work would make me super fit at the very least and yet I look a wreck.'

'Why does it matter so much?' I said sternly.

'Of course it matters,' Jo snapped, rinsing. 'I haven't quite given up on myself yet. I don't want to go round looking so dirty and disgusting that people in the streets run away from me screaming.'

'You don't mind what you look like when you go out to the supermarket,' I said.

'Well at that time most people have their eyes tightly closed – even the ones that are up,' said Jo, sluicing more water over herself and then getting up. 'Pass us that towel and stop being so stupid.'

'You're the one that's being stupid in my opinion,' I said. 'You don't care what you look like when you go to the Rosens' either, you just wear any old gungy thing. You don't care what you look like when you go and collect Robin from school and bring him back here. But suddenly, when it's time to take him home to his dad, it's flap and fuss and you getting worked up into a right flap-doodle.'

'I don't know what you're on about,' said Jo, towelling herself dry.

'Yes you do. What's the matter with you, Jo? Why are you trying to impress that wimpy little kid's father, eh?'

'I'm not. I just want him to see he's got a competent and reasonably clean person looking after his son. Stop looking so *fierce*, Charlie.'

'But you like him, don't you?' I asked.

'I don't even know him properly. He's just my employer.'

'You're not going to do anything really gross and go out with him, are you?' I said.

'Oooh, now, that's a great idea,' said Jo. 'And you and your Jamie could come too on a double date, how about that?'

'You shut up teasing me. I'm serious!' I said. 'I'm having grave doubts about you, Loopy Mum. We don't like men, remember? *Especially* the lean lost ones. Honestly! What a description. You are a *fool*.'

'Don't you tell me I'm a fool. I'm your mother!' said Jo, trying to act all dignified. 'Now go and keep an eye on poor little Robin and stop bugging me. Do as you're told!'

'Who's going to make me? You and whose army?' I said, standing my ground.

'Go!' said Jo, giving me a push.

'No!' I said, giving her a push back.

'You do as I say,' said Jo, pushing with both hands.

'I don't want to,' I said, pushing back.

We went on pushing and shoving and Jo's towel fell off and she tried to grab it and I snatched it first and slipped on the bath mat and Jo fell on top of me and we rolled around, starting to giggle as we wrestled.

'Oh!' said a little voice.

 We looked up and there was Robin at the bath-room door, his mouth open in astonishment.

'Sorry, Robin!' said Jo, grabbing the towel back and wrapping it round herself.

'Are you fighting?' Robin enquired timidly.

'Yes,' I said.

'No, of course we're not,' said Jo. 'Take no notice of Charlie, Robin. She's a wild child, totally out of my control.'

'Grrrrrr!' I said, baring my teeth dramatically.

'Will she fight me?' Robin asked.

'No, of course she won't, she's only teasing,' said Jo.

'Yes, I will,' I said, and I swooped on him and picked him up under his armpits and swung him round wildly so that his spindly legs kicked in the air.

He squealed noisily but he seemed to be enjoying it.

'Stop being so rough with him,' Jo called, pulling on her clothes in the bedroom.

'Is he lean and lost like his daddy then?' I said, setting Robin back on his feet. His face was flushed robin red, his eyes dark with excitement. He took a step and staggered. I caught hold of him.

'It's OK, you're just giddy,' I said as he clung to me. His hands were like little monkey paws. I wondered if he'd ever clung to his mum the way he was clinging to me.

'Giddy,' Robin repeated. This was obviously a new experience for him. He moved tentatively.

'There, it's getting better, isn't it? Hey, did you put all the tops back on my felt tip pens, yeah?'

'Oh yes. Honest,' said Robin.

'Did you do a drawing?'

'I started.'

'Let's see then.' I walked him over to the kitchen table. He'd drawn a very big Birdie as I'd suggested, with a tiny Robin clinging to his back. They were just landing in the Magic Land, Birdie's wings outstretched. I touched the strip of green below Birdie's claws. 'Is this the Magic Land then?' I asked.

Robin nodded. 'Yes! Shall I draw it for you, Charlie?'

'OK. Go on then. What's in your Magic Land, eh? Pink candy-floss trees and rivers with tame dolphins and unicorns you can ride and it's never ever bedtime?' I suggested, trying to conjure up a dinky little Magic Land that might take his fancy.

Jo and I elaborated endlessly on our own Magic Lands. It was one of our favourite games. Jo's current Magic Land was a huge turquoise swimming pool and she'd float endlessly on a white lilo sipping champagne and eating white cream chocolates all day long.

My special Magic Land was an immense jungle and I'd hack my way through, not the slightest bit scared even when huge pythons wound themselves round my waist or tigers roared at me or elephants suddenly charged. I'd whistle a magic tune so that the python swayed in a hypnotic trance, I'd roar right back at the tiger, and I'd catch hold of the elephant's trunk and get him to lift me up on his head between his mighty ears and we'd thunder across the land together.

I started drawing my own Magic Land, concentrating on the immensely tall trees, home of great gorillas and hairy orang-utans and tribes of funny furry monkeys, and I was Queen of all the Apes and swung through the trees faster than any of them.

'Look, this is my Magic Land. See the monkeys?' I said, showing Robin.

He was kneeling up on his chair, drawing intently, his tongue sticking out he was concentrating so hard. I peered at his picture.

'That's not a Magic Land!' I said. 'You're just drawing your mum and your dad again.'

'Yes, they're in my Magic Land, and we all live there and it's magic,' said Robin. He bent his head very near his drawing, as if he was trying to step inside it.

'It's nearly time we were off, Robin. We'll show Daddy your lovely picture, yes?' said Jo.

That wasn't all they were going to show off to Daddy. Jo was wearing her shortest skirt and her little angora wool jumper. I usually call her Fluffy Bunny when she wears it. I didn't at all feel like flattering her with babyish nicknames now. What was she *doing*, getting all dolled up to deliver little Robin back home? She was supposed to do some housework when she was there too, so why dress up like she was going dating, not dusting?

'What?' said Jo, all wide-eyed, as I glared at her.

'You know what,' I said.

She was hours getting back home too. Well, an hour late. Just over half an hour. But she was still *late*.

'What are you playing at, eh?' I said furiously.

Jo burst out laughing.

'It's not funny!' I exploded.

'Yes it is. Talk about role reversal. Watch it, Charlie. You're starting to sound just like Grandma. "Why are you so late back, Josephine? This simply isn't good enough. And wipe that smirk off your face, it's not funny."'

'Well, maybe if you'd listened to Grandma instead of thinking you knew best then you wouldn't have ended up as a single parent having to go out cleaning for other people to keep a roof over our heads,' I said.

There was a sudden silence. We were both shocked. Jo's never minded if I shout back at her but I've never tried to hurt her like that before. I put my hand over my lips to try to get them under control.

Jo was struggling too, no longer laughing. 'OK. Maybe that's a good point – if a cheap one. Though I'm glad I made that major mistake because I got you out of it. And you're the best thing that's ever happened to me, even if you're acting like a right old ratbag at this present moment in time,' said Jo. 'I'm sorry if you were worried I was late. I didn't realize. Mark and I just got talking and—'

'So it's Mark, is it?'

'Oh come off it, Charlie. He's not the sort of man you call Mr Reed.'

'No, he's the little-boy-lost type, yeah?'

'I don't know why you're being so *stupid*,' said Jo. 'You're acting like I'm going out with him or something.'

'Well – don't you want to?'

'Of course not. He's my employer. He's a nice quiet friendly man who adores his son and he's still hurting after the break up of his marriage and he's lonely and he just likes to talk a bit, that's all. And – and – I like to talk to him too.'

'Why? You're not lonely. You've got me.'

Jo looked as if she might giggle again. 'You're sounding like my husband now!'

'Well, why do you have to get all prettied up in your best clothes just to talk to this Mark?'

'*Definitely* like a husband. Oh, Charlie!' Jo put her arms round me, her angora tickling my cheeks.

'Get off. You're getting fluff all over me,' I said, sneezing.

'Well, stop being such a prize berk, eh? Look, if it keeps you happy I'll tell Mark tomorrow that I'm not allowed to say another word to him because it annoys my fierce bossy man-hating daughter.'

'Right, you do that,' I said.

I knew I was being ridiculous. But I couldn't help it.

I was fed up at school too. Angela and Lisa were being stupid stupid stupid. Angela had joined this dippy fan club and had a special magazine and a signed photo of her new favourites and a T-shirt with all their heads on which she wore every day under her school shirt. She endlessly read aloud the most amazingly trivial facts about her new darlings, like one had a thing about red-and-white striped toothpaste and another had a wacky Scottish auntie and another fell about laughing every time he saw Bugs Bunny. Well, so what??? But Angela kept giving great excited whoops and yelling, 'Listen to this, listen to this!'

Lisa was getting pretty cheesed off with this too, but she was just as bad over Dave Wood. Worse even. She went bright red whenever he came remotely near her, and when one day in singing the music teacher had her standing right next to Dave, Lisa was so overcome she couldn't sing a note, she just opened and shut her mouth like a goldfish.

'I was so *embarrassed*,' she kept saying afterwards. 'I mean, we were practically touching.'

'Yuck! I wouldn't touch Dave Wood with a bargepole,' I said.

'Oh *you*,' said Lisa. 'Look, do you think Dave likes me?'

'*I* don't know,' I said impatiently. 'Why don't you ask him?'

'I can't *ask* him! No, I've got to find some subtle way of finding out.'

'I'll ask him, if you like,' said Angela, reaching down her school blouse and blowing kisses to the faces on her T-shirt.

'No, that's not subtle enough,' said Lisa.

'Angela, stop doing that, it looks seriously weird,' I said. 'And you're trying to be so subtle it's just a waste of space. Never mind whether that twerp likes you. He most likely doesn't have a clue that *you* like *him*.'

'Well, I can't tell him that!' said Lisa.

'Why not? Though *how* you can like him I just can't fathom. I can't stand the way his hair flops forward into his eyes so that he has to keep flipping it out the way!'

'I think that's seriously cute,' said Lisa.

'Yuck!'

'Yes, double yuck,' said Angela, giving me hope, but then she started on about the hairstyles of all her pop darlings until I was ready to tear out *my* hair. In fact I got so seriously bored that I stalked off by myself.

I was feeling so fed up that when some stupid boys kicked their football and hit me right on the head I found I had tears in my eyes. I blinked rapidly, horrified. I never ever cried at school, no matter what. Even when I was a little kid right back in Year One and some big boys gave me a Chinese burn I didn't cry.

SMACK!

'Watch it, you stupid idiots,' I said, and I took their football and threw it as far away as I could, right over behind the bike sheds.

'Oh, you rotten pig, why did you go and do that?' they groaned. 'What's up with you, Cakehole? Just because you've had a tiff with your little girly gang there's no need to take it out on us.'

I responded with a very rude gesture. Miss Beckworth was on playground duty. I hoped she hadn't seen. I made off sharpish in the opposite direction, dodging behind the Portakabins.

Jamie Edwards was sitting on the steps, head deep in a book. He looked startled when he saw me – but he smiled nervously.

'You still reading about that Esther?' I said.

'I finished that book ages ago. I read ever so quickly,' said Jamie, unable to resist a little boast.

'So what you reading now then, eh?' I peered at the densely printed pages. 'It looks even worse. Ever so hard.'

'Ever so Hardy,' said Jamie, chuckling, showing me the spine.

'*Tess of the D'Urbervilles* by Thomas Hardy – oh, I get you, ha ha, very droll. It sounds awful! Is it French with that funny name?'

'No. It's English, about this girl Tess and she goes to work on a farm and this man has his wicked way with her,' said Jamie, eyes gleaming.

'Oh, another one of *those*. You are awful, Jamie.'

'And it's ever so sad, because Tess has a baby and then she falls in love again but it all goes wrong and I know it's not going to have a happy ending.'

'Oh, hang about! I've seen it on the telly, I think. There's a bit about Stonehenge at the end – I watched it with Jo and we both wept buckets.'

'Is Jo your sister?'

'No, my mum.'

'And you're allowed to call her by her first name?'

'I can call her whatever I like,' I said.

I felt like inventing some new and incredibly nasty names for her because I was still so annoyed with her. I kept thinking about her with this creep Mark. I didn't know what he looked like, so I imagined him like Robin but big. A *total* wimp. So why why why did Jo want to bound round to his house in her bunny jumper and twitch her nose at him?

Mark?

'Are you planning to go round to Lisa's or Angela's on Friday night?' Jo said that evening.

'Maybe. I don't know. I've got a bit fed up with them recently,' I said gloomily, chucking my school copy of *Victorian Life* on the floor. None of Miss Beckworth's books went into the sort of detail I wanted. 'I might just go round to Jamie's house because he keeps telling me he's got all these Victorian books he'll lend me.'

'Oh, round to Jamie's house, eh?' said Jo.

'So?' I said fiercely. 'It's just to borrow a book.'

'OK, OK. But if you stay for tea or anything, can his mum or dad run you home? I can't come and fetch you because . . . I'm babysitting for Robin.'

I stared at her. So Mark was going out?

'Who's this Mark going out with?' I asked.

Jo shrugged uneasily. 'I don't know. Look, he just asked if I could – could come round and babysit, so I said OK, but I won't be back late, and I can always say no if it's not all right with you, Charlie.'

'It's fine with me,' I said. It obviously wasn't fine with Jo. I felt a bit sorry for her. But I was also thrilled for me. The wimp had got himself some girlfriend so he couldn't be interested in Jo. He just wanted her to look after little Robin.

Or so I thought.

I was so stupid! I didn't twig at all. Not that first Friday, or even the Friday after. I was so pleased and relieved I was extra nice to Jo.

We had a wonderful Sunday, having a really long lie in and then a dozy hour or two snuggled up in bed playing Magic Lands and then, when we eventually got up, I made us special little fairy cakes. We ate them hot out of the oven for breakfast and then later when they'd cooled down I iced them pink and then changed to white in my little icing bag and piped funny messages over them – HELLO and I LIKE YOU and FUNNY FACE – like those little love heart sweets.

I took them to school the next morning. There was a lot of silly teasing about Cakehole making cakes – but everyone seemed dead impressed when they saw them. Everyone wanted one, but they were only for a select few. I gave Lisa an I LIKE YOU and told her what to do with it. She giggled and blushed and protested and wouldn't give it to Dave Wood outright – but he saw her leave it on his desk, so the message got through.

I gave Angela another I LIKE YOU and she pretend-fed it to the grinning faces on her T-shirt and then gobbled it up herself.

I gave more cakes to the girls I'd liked best in our old gang, and then Lisa and Angela and I had another two each. There was just one left by the time we went back into school.

'Did you make those little cakes yourself, Charlie?' Jamie asked.

'Yup.'

'They looked ever so nice. Really tasty,' said Jamie wistfully.

I looked at him. And then I sighed and reached in the tin and gave him the last one. It didn't say HELLO. It didn't say FUNNY FACE. It said I LIKE YOU.

COURTSHIP

It was bitterly cold in the park today. Louisa cried because she could not feel her feet inside her boots and baby Freddie's nose kept running in a most unattractive way. Victor ran ahead with his hoop to get warm, so I stuck Louisa into the pram beside Freddie and ran too. We raced all the way home, careering round the corner and practically running over the butcher's boy. He did not seem to mind.

'Whoops—a—blooming—buttercup!' he said. 'Mind what you're doing with that perambulator, Miss. It's a dangerous weapon!'

No—one has ever called *me* Miss before. I must admit I liked it, though I stuck my nose in the air and called the butcher's boy a saucepot.

Trust Victor to hang back at that precise moment. 'What were you saying to that errand boy, Charlotte?' he enquired.

'It's none of your business, Master Victor,' I said haughtily.

'Is he going to be your gentleman caller?' Victor asked.

'Certainly not!' I said, and I took Victor's hoop and bowled it so hard he had to run like the wind to stop it going into the road and under a carriage.

That settled his hash. He well knows that his mamma does not allow the servants to have gentleman callers. I had to protect Eliza when she was canoodling in the kitchen with her current sweetheart, the draper's assistant, who had come to deliver the Mistress's new shawl and gloves. In finest cashmere. If only I had a warm woolly shawl and mittens! I have chilblains that throb and itch like the devil.

Anyway, I was down in the kitchen fetching the children's hot milk and biscuits when I heard the Mistress clip-clopping down the stairs in her neat kid boots.

'Quick, Eliza, the Mistress is coming!' I hissed, and then I bounded *up* the stairs and waylaid the Mistress by telling her a very long story about Miss Louisa—not—drinking—her—milk—even—though—it's—so—good—for—her, and by the time I'd done and the Mistress had made her way down to the kitchen Eliza had had time to bundle any number of gentlemen callers out of the back door.

She didn't say anything to me, but Eliza and Mrs Angel stopped calling me Baby and laughing behind my back — and yesterday when the children were asleep Eliza slipped into the nursery with a bowl of Mrs Angel's special sherry trifle for my supper.

Mrs Angel is Mother's age but she has gentlemen callers too! The fat policeman for the street calls on a regular basis for his piece of pie and Mrs Angel's patter. I was astonished to see a woman so old go rosy-cheeked and chuckle when he praised her pastry.

I received a letter from Rose today and now I am starting to worry that Mother herself might be courting!!! Rose says that Mr Higgins from the Dog and Duck brings Mother a jug of ale from time to time, and in return she cooks him a meal. I do not like the sound of this!

Rose's letter makes me feel *so* homesick. It is a poor ill-spelt half-page but I have read it as avidly as if it were a masterpiece by Mr Dickens. Rose has never tried hard enough at school. She writes that Miss Worthbeck sends her kindest regards and can scarce manage without me. And a certain Edward James sends a most impertinent message to Dear Little Lottie. Hmm!

SUNDAY

I found it seriously weird going round to Jamie's house. I mean, this was Jamie Edwards, the worst boy in the whole class, old chubby-chops super-swot wimpy-wuss Jamie. I made pretty sure all the boys in our class treated me with respect but I wanted a capital 'R' from Jamie.

Yet in his huge great famously Victorian villa he was so different. As if he'd grown to fit his fourteen-roomed house. (I counted.) And I felt different too. As if I'd shrunk considerably. It felt strange just going into his house through that dark-blue front door with the big brass lion knocker. I felt as if I should slink round the back or down the basement steps like my Lottie.

If Jamie and his family had lorded it over me I'd somehow have felt easier. I could just dismiss them as horrible snobs and sneer at them. But they were ever so friendly. Even Jamie's elder brother Jules.

Elder brothers are usually a race apart. Angela's elder brother charges straight past you without even bothering to say hello. He doesn't even mean to be rude, it's just that you don't register with him. But Jules said Hi and chatted like I was his age and he made me and Jamie a toasted sandwich. We ate it in the kitchen – but *what* a kitchen! I stared round, scarcely able to swallow.

There was a shelf of cookery books and I had a quick peer but I couldn't see anything special on cakes. When Jamie's mum got home much later I saw she wasn't really a cake-maker. She came in 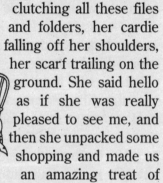 clutching all these files and folders, her cardie falling off her shoulders, her scarf trailing on the ground. She said hello as if she was really pleased to see me, and then she unpacked some shopping and made us an amazing treat of cream cheese and smoked salmon in a strange round roll. (No wonder Jamie is chubby round his chops with all these delicious snacks on offer.) Jules had one of these bagel things too, and then went up to his room to get on with his homework.

All Jamie's family are seriously brainy. Jules is going to take *twelve* GCSEs, and then there are two older brothers, both at university. Jamie's mum and dad *lecture* at the university. He teaches French, she teaches Politics and Economics.

'The Economics is a bit of a laugh,' said Jamie.

'Mum can hardly add up. She's meant to pay me when I do stuff like vacuuming and that, two quid an hour, plus appropriate percentage for ten minutes extra, say, and *can* she work it out? Nope! Clueless, aren't you, Mum?'

I didn't think his mum clueless at all, paying Jamie a measly two quid per hour when the rock-bottom going rate was £3.50 and the Rosens right next door paid Jo a fiver an hour – dead Economical! Things got a bit awkward when Jamie's mum started chatting about how she remembered me from way back when I had my hair in a pony tail (yuck!) and then she said: 'And you always looked so cute because your big sister had a pony tail too, so you both walked along to the school, hair bobbing away.'

I smiled in a strained sort of way and decided to keep my mouth shut. But Jamie didn't.

'Oh, Mum, honestly! That wasn't Charlie's sister. She's her mum.'

Jamie's mum looked startled. 'Good Heavens! Oh Charlie, what a lovely young mum you've got! Not an old bag like me, eh? What does your mum do?'

I swallowed. 'Well . . . she used to be sort of a lecturer like you.' It was true in a way. She was always having to give her staff a right lecture in her shop.

'So now . . . ?'

'Now she's – well, she's been made redundant, I mean, it's not her fault, she didn't get the sack or anything, it's just—'

'Oh, tell me about it! We're in a sticky situation at

115

the moment too. We're all very worried. So has your mother found another post at all?'

'Well. Not – not lecturing. She's having to do temporary work.'

'I see. Well, I do hope things sort themselves out soon for her. Is it . . . ?' She paused delicately, trying very hard not to put her foot in it again. 'Is it just your mother and you at home?'

'Yes.'

Just Jo and me in a home we're hanging on to by the skin of our teeth. If Jamie's mum loses her posh job then they'll maybe have to swop from smoked salmon to tinned, but they'll still be able to live in their huge great house. OK, they have actually got a couple of lodgers right upstairs, two students from the university. They've got a bedroom each, a shared living room and kitchenette, and their own bathroom and loo. The students' rooms are bigger than our flat.

It still leaves the Edwards with so many different rooms. This includes a *library*. They've got books in absolutely every room, even the downstairs loo, and there are shelves in the hall and the living room downstairs, but there's this huge great room on the first floor absolutely crammed full of books, and there are shelves and shelves of Victorian stuff.

'See,' said Jamie proudly, pulling various volumes down and displaying them in front of me.

I saw. No wonder Jamie's Victorian project was

116

so brilliant. Still, he was letting me look at the books if I wanted.

'You've still got time to do a proper project instead of that old diary thing,' he said. Unwisely.

'Cheek! I don't want to do a boring old project. Who wants to be like everyone else? I'm doing my diary – and yes it is "old", it's *supposed* to be old, it's meant to be written by a Victorian, for goodness' sake.'

'OK, OK. You don't have to get all heavy with me,' said Jamie. 'You're so fierce, Charlie.'

'Fierce?' I said. I said it again, savouring the word. I felt as if he'd paid me a real compliment.

'So don't you want to borrow any of the Victorian books, then? Because we can go and play a game on my computer if you want. Or I'll show you my dinosaur stuff. Or we can play War.'

'War? You mean fight?' I said, grinning. 'I know who's going to win.'

'No, it's a game, with all these little soldiers – *they* fight, and there are little guns and land mines and all that stuff. It's great to play but Jules won't play it with me, neither will Mum or Dad or anyone because they're all pacifists.'

'I'm not. I'll play you. But just let me look at this book a tick.'

I'd found a whole set of Victorian girls' books. I wanted to see if there might be any Lottie could have read. There was one huge fat annual with lots of pictures, like a magazine. There was one coloured picture of a huge table groaning with wobbly jellies

 and puddings like castles and all sorts of dinky sweets and teeny sandwiches . . . and fancy cakes.

'Hey, look! I just want to take a couple of notes, OK?'

'OK. Though why don't you borrow it?'

'You mean I can take it home with me?'

'Sure.'

'Oh. Well. Great.' I tucked the huge book under my arm. 'So let's play War.'

We played War for hours. It was a great game. And guess who won!

Jamie's mum ran me home in her car. I was worried she might object about the book because it was probably valuable as it's so old but she didn't turn a hair. Her hair is already grey. I wonder what it's like to have a mum old enough to be your granny. I think it's much more fun to have a mum young enough to be your sister.

'We've heard so much about you, Charlie,' said Jamie's mum.

I blinked.

'You've made a big impression on Jamie,' she said.

I thought about it. I'd made a *literal* impression on Jamie several times.

'We're going to the V and A on Sunday afternoon,' she said.

'The what?'

'Sorry. The Victoria and Albert Museum. I know Jamie would love it if you'd come with us – and it would be very useful for this famous Victorian project.'

'Well. Thank you very much. But Sunday is sort of special. Jo and I do things together.'

'She's very welcome to come too.'

'Thanks, but . . . I don't think we can.'

'Well, another time maybe. And do come round to our house any time you want. It'd be lovely to see you,' said Jamie's mum.

I was a little bit dubious. Did Jamie have an actual thing about me? He hadn't acted all lovey-dovey when we were in his room. The mere thought of Jamie Edwards acting lovey-dovey was enough to crease me up. Just let him try! And anyway, I didn't want to go to some stuffy old museum on a Sunday. Like I said, Sundays were just for Jo and me.

So I was utterly shocked and stupefied when Jo dropped this ginormous bombshell.

'We're going out on Sunday,' she said.

'Oh yeah?'

'How would you like to go to Red River Theme Park?' she said.

I stared at her. I'd been wanting to go to Red River ever since it opened. Lisa had promised she'd get her dad to take Angela and me for her birthday treat, but that wasn't until next year. And it wasn't a certainty anyway, because it cost a fortune to get into Red River.

'We can't afford it,' I said to Jo.

'We're being taken out,' she said. 'Isn't it great?'

'*Who's* taking us out?' I said, starting to smell a rat. A great big rat with twitchy whiskers on its lean lost face. And I was spot on.

'Mark was talking about taking Robin this Sunday and he thought it would be so much more fun if we all went together. He's paying, and I'm getting a picnic together. It's going to be a fantastic day out.'

'We don't have days out on Sundays. We have days in. Just you and me. As a matter of fact, *I* was asked out on Sunday, the Edwards family asked me, they wanted to take me out for this bumper day in London, a drive all round the sights and lunch in Planet Hollywood and then this museum for Victorian stuff and then tea at one of those really posh hotels, scones and cream cakes and all that, and then – then we were going for dinner at the Hard Rock Café and – and *then*—'

'Then you were going to be violently sick, I should think,' said Jo. She reached out and ran her finger up and down my lips, the way you do a baby to make it go wibble-wibble-wibble. 'This is a bad mouth,' said Jo. 'It is telling fibs.'

'They did ask me out on Sunday, honest,' I insisted.

'Well, you can't, because I've already said we're going to Red River with Mark and Robin,' said Jo. 'Come *on*, Charlie! You've been desperate to go to Red River for ages. I thought you'd be over the moon. I think it's absolutely great of Mark to invite us.'

'Why us, though? Why isn't he going with this girlfriend of his?' I said.

'What girlfriend?' said Jo. She frowned.

'The one he's started seeing on Friday nights when you babysit,' I said.

'Oh. I see. Ah,' said Jo.

'What?' I said. *'What?'* Although I suddenly *knew* what.

'I think you maybe got hold of the wrong end of the stick,' said Jo. 'I never said Mark had a girlfriend.'

'So where did he go when you went round to babysit?'

'Well . . . the first Friday he was going out, just to see this film he fancied, but we got chatting, and then we watched this film together on the telly instead, so—'

'So you're the one who's been telling dirty great lies,' I said.

'No I'm not!'

'And *you're* his girlfriend now, aren't you?' I said.

'Of course I'm not. Don't be so silly. I'm not Mark's girlfriend. I work for him. I've only known him a few weeks. Oh, Charlie, don't be so difficult.'

I felt like being difficult. I was Mega Mad. No-one seemed to understand why. Lisa and Angela and I went round the shops on Saturday afternoon and they thought I was completely nuts.

'Can't you get this guy to take us too?' said Lisa hopefully. 'Say we're your all-time best friends and you can't go without us. After all, I promised I'd get my dad to take you two on my birthday.'

'This guy isn't my dad though. He isn't anything. He's just this creep who's started chatting up my mother.'

'Still, who cares if he's a creep? You still get to go to Red River,' said Lisa.

'Yeah, I'll go in your place if you don't want to,' said Angela. 'I just go to church on Sundays. You count yourself lucky, Charlie.'

'No, you've got to be a good girl and go to church,' said Lisa. '*I'll* go instead of Charlie. I just have to go to all these boring antique fairs with my mum while my dad plays golf, it's not fair.'

'Neither of you are going,' I said. 'And *I'm* not going too.'

I told Jo that on Saturday evening, while she was busy getting all this picnic stuff together.

'OK,' said Jo, mashing up hard-boiled eggs.

'I really mean it. I'm not going. And you can't make me,' I said.

'Right,' said Jo, mashing harder.

'So that's settled,' I said.

'Yep,' said Jo, pounding so hard that the bowl rattled.

'I'm not going to Granny's or anything. I'll just stay here. By myself. I'll be fine,' I said.

'Aha,' said Jo, and her hand slipped and she banged it hard on the edge of the kitchen top. She bent over, clutching her wrist.

'You're not supposed to mash like that. You're hopeless when it comes to cooking,' I said. 'Jo?'

She didn't answer this time. Her head was so bent I couldn't see her face for hair. I went over to her. I saw a tear trickling down her cheek.

'I've really upset you, haven't I?' I said.

'No. I've just hurt my wrist, that's all,' said Jo.

She can be as stubborn as me sometimes. Her wrist wasn't really hurt. And she stopped crying when I put my arms round her and told her that I would go to Red River on Sunday if she really really really wanted me to go.

I even made some more little fairy cakes for the picnic. With messages.

Mark was exactly how I imagined him. No, worse. The sort of bumbling Bambi-eyed boy-man that makes some women go bananas. He had a tuft of hair sticking up on top and little round glasses and a big check shirt and faded jeans and one of his socks was black and the other was navy. *Pathetic*. Mark almost made little Robin look macho. He was ever so scared of me. 'Hi, Charlie,' he said, trying to sound dead casual, but he stuttered – and when he attempted this silly little wave, spreading his fingers, I saw his palm was all sweaty. Yuck.

But there was something far far worse. Jo. She was better at acting cool, of course. If you didn't know her you'd think she was dead relaxed, making a fuss of Robin and flappy little Birdie, chatting nineteen to the dozen to Mark, telling some silly story about her supermarket job, the day her machine ran away with her and attacked a pile of loo rolls. I don't think it even happened, she was just making it up as she went along, but it made Mark laugh and even little Robin tittered behind Birdie's wing. But she was just pretending all the time, her voice too high, her eyes blinking, her hands gesticulating wildly. She was like a clockwork toy that had been wound up too tightly.

I yawned and started humming to myself while she was in mid-flow to show her I wasn't impressed. I hardly said a word the entire car journey to Red River Theme Park. Jo was going jabber jabber jabber so there was no point anyway.

Mark seemed so impressed that he could barely keep his eyes on the road ahead. 'Yeah? Mmm? *Really?*' he'd go, and every so often he'd crack up laughing.

I slumped back in my seat, weary with this deeply disgusting performance. Mark caught sight of me in his driving mirror. 'Are you all right, Charlie?' he said.

I didn't bother to reply.

'She's not feeling sick, is she?' Mark asked Jo.

Jo turned round. 'Stop being a pig,' she mouthed at me.

I gave one small snort for her

benefit. Robin blinked at me in surprise.

'She's OK,' said Jo.

'And you're OK too, Robin?' Mark asked. 'You don't feel sick or anything?'

'I don't think so,' Robin mumbled. 'But maybe Birdie does a bit.'

Oh great. I didn't care for the idea of Robin chucking up all over me.

'Talk to Robin, Charlie,' said Jo. 'Take his mind off it.'

I didn't want to talk to Robin. Or his dad. Or my stupid mother, all got up in her fluffy pink top and her tiny skirt. To match her new shrunk tiny brain and her fluffy pink persona. Bimbo Mum. Out with Bambi Man and Birdie Boy.

'What's *up* with you, Charlie?' Jo said, her voice sharp.

There was nothing up with me. I was the only person in the car acting anywhere near normal.

'She's shy,' said Mark.

Me, shy! I snorted again.

'She's not shy,' said Jo. 'Are you, Charlie? I'm the one who always gets into states about things and can hardly say boo to a goose. Charlie's always had far more guts than me. She was born a fighter, eh, Charlie?'

She was sucking up to me now. It was sickening. Robin seemed to find it sickening too. Literally.

'Birdie's starting to feel *very* sick,' he gasped, his face pale green.

I snapped into action mega fast, opening his

window and sticking his little head out just in time. He was sick all over the car, but at least it was outside, not inside. We had to pull up in a lay-by and get him mopped up and the car wiped down. I backed away from both these proceedings. As Mark had to deal with the car Jo had to sluice the sicky dribble off Robin. She's always had a weak stomach. Still, she was the one who wanted to play Happy Families. Let her be Mother.

Robin started wimpering that he smelt, and eventually Jo had to waste a bottle of the picnic water washing him. Then Robin snivelled that Birdie smelt too, because one tiny tip of his wing had got stained. Birdie had to have a regular little bird-bath too.

I was practically at screaming point by the time we drove off in the car. The day didn't improve. The world and his wife had decided to visit the Red River Theme Park. We were not the world and we certainly weren't ever going to be anyone's wife, but we were stuck in their traffic jam. It took hours before we got there, and then there was a huge queue to park and by the time we staggered through the entrance we felt as exhausted as if we'd already had a day out.

Still, I decided I might as well make the most of this opportunity and I clamoured straight away to go on the really scary famous Red River Run.

'Let's go a bit gently first,' said Jo. 'Robin still looks a bit pale. What would you like to go on, Robin?'

He twittered and skittered and eventually decided

he wanted to try the Treetops ride because Birdie might see a lot of big birds up there. I was getting heartily sick of all this twee Birdie nonsense by now. I wished Birdie would flap his wings and fly away, sharpish.

We went on this Treetops ride and it was a bit babyish because you rode round this aerial scenic railway ever so slowly, absolutely no swooping up and down or looping-the-looping. Big birds were very few on the ground too. Well, few in the air, shall we say. I'd have stuck stuffed parrots to every branch and dangled a few eagles in the air just to make the view a bit livelier. You couldn't rely on the real birds to put on an entertaining aerial display. A few sparrows flapped far away and that was our lot.

It was all very tame. For me. Not for Robin. He went a familiar pale green.

'Put your head over the side of the truck,' I said quickly.

But when he did as he was told he looked down *through* the treetops and got so scared he couldn't even be sick (which was just as well for all the unsuspecting folk wandering around underneath!) Robin just opened his mouth and screamed.

'Hey, Robin! It's OK, son. Don't yell like that. It's meant to be fun,' said Mark, turning round and trying to put his arms round him.

'Don't look down, Robin.

Look up at the trees. Look, there's a pigeon,' said Jo.

'Can't anyone shut him up?' I said. 'Robin, you're giving Birdie a headache. Look, he's had to put his head under his wing. Shut up, OK?'

It wasn't OK. He didn't shut up until we'd finished the ride and hauled him off. Mark picked him up and he buried his head in his shirt and gradually adjusted the scream to an intermittent sob.

'Well, he's having a whale of a time,' I said.

Jo gave me a shove. 'Will you stop being so hateful?' she hissed. 'Poor little Robin.'

'Yes, poor little wimpy-pimpy,' I said. 'Come on, Jo. He's not a baby. He's five, for goodness' sake. In Victorian times he'd be old enough to shove up a chimney.'

'I wish I could shove you up a chimney,' said Jo. 'Look, he acts like a baby because his mum's cleared off and he feels like his whole world has fallen apart. Can't you understand?'

I was starting to feel that way myself. Like my own mum had cleared off. Jo turned her back on me and started fuss fuss fussing over Robin, and all the time Mark was looking at her with this sickening soft expression so that now I was the one who felt like throwing up.

Robin wouldn't go on any other rides, apart from a twiddly little roundabout for tiny tots. He sat bolt upright in a little car and held on to that steering wheel so tightly his knuckles were practically bursting out of his skin. Jo and Mark waved like crazy every time he came round but he never once looked at them. He stared straight ahead, as if he were watching the road.

He wanted another go. And another.

'Look, this is loopy,' I pointed out. 'It costs a fortune to get in and you're supposed to go on all these incredible rides and all we're doing is watching Robin go round and round a roundabout that would only cost fifty pence at a summer fête.'

'At least he's liking it,' said Jo.

'But this is his last go. I agree with you, Charlie. Hey, we'll go on the Red River Ride, eh, you and me?' said Mark.

I couldn't stand the way he was trying so hard to get on with me.

'I'll go on my own, thanks,' I said.

But for some infuriating reason they didn't let kids under twelve ride on their own.

'You come, Jo. Go on. Please,' I said, practically begging.

But it was no use. I ended up surfing the Red River with Mark. It spoilt it all utterly. People seeing us together might have thought he was my *dad*. I sat as far away from him as I possibly could. He kept yelling, 'Isn't this fun! Isn't this great!' though he'd gone almost as green as his son. When we lurched up to the very top and then swooped down like crazy he screamed so that I could see the fillings in his back teeth. When we got to the last and largest hill of steel before the watersplash he actually tried to put his arm round me.

'Do you mind?' I said, and I wriggled as far away as I could just as we went over the top. My head jerked forward as I hurtled down and I banged my nose hard on the safety bar. Pain exploded in my head as water splashed right over us and soaked us to the skin.

'Wow!' said Mark. 'Hey, Charlie, what's up? Did you bump your head? Your poor nose is all red.'

'No. I'm fine,' I said thickly, trying to blink my tears back.

I didn't want his soggy sympathy. Even though it was all his fault. Him and his silly snivelly son.

Jo was still so busy fussing over Robin that she didn't even *notice* that my nose had suddenly turned into a tomato. So I decided I wouldn't bother to tell her. Even though it was more than likely broken, and my looks would be marred for all time.

We went to the picnic area but I wasn't really hungry. My nose throbbed so much and chewing aggravated it. The picnic wasn't up to much anyway. The sandwiches had gone limp inside and hard out because Jo had made them the night before. She'd packed the crisps under the cans of Coke so that they were all broken into little bits. The grapes had got so squashed that one more trample would have turned them into wine.

The only good part of the picnic were my fairy cakes which I'd packed myself in a nest of paper tissues inside a big tin. They were delicious. And carefully iced with witty messages. I handed them round so that everyone got the right one.

Mine said HEY, BEAUTIFUL.

Jo's said TRAITOR.

Mark's said DEADLY POISON.

Robin's said GET LOST.

'What does it mean, g-e-t l-o-s-t?' said Robin, licking his message tentatively.

'Oh, it's just Charlie being silly,' said Jo, glaring at me. She didn't even touch her cake. Mark gave a great false roar of laughter and ate his in two gulps.

'Yum yum, delicious,' he said, and then he gasped and pretended to choke.

'Daddy?' said Robin.

'It's OK, Daddy's just dying,' I said.

'It's a silly joke, Robin,' said Jo, cramming the lid back on the rest of the cakes. She looked like she wanted to cram me inside too. Without any airholes. 'How would you like another go on that little round-about, Robin?'

He had many more goes. And I went on some other rides too, but somehow they all seemed a waste of time. My whole head was hurting now, not just my nose. Sometimes I went on the rides with

Mark while Jo looked after Robin. Sometimes I went on the rides with Jo. That wasn't any better, because we weren't speaking.

Then we got to the Stardust Sparkle ride. It was all pink glitter and hearts and flowers outside.

'That's pretty,' said Robin.

'Pretty yucky,' I said.

'Would you like to go on the Stardust Sparkle ride, Robin?' said Jo. 'We could all go on it, eh?'

Robin watched the ride warily. A couple got into a pink pretend Cadillac and it drove through a door in the shape of a big heart. You couldn't see inside the door. It was all dark.

'No,' said Robin. 'Too dark. I don't like the dark.'

'Surprise surprise,' I said. 'Well, *I* certainly don't want to go on the Stardust Sparkle ride either, if anybody's interested. Not that anyone is.'

'I'd like to,' said Mark. 'Come on, Jo.'

I stared at her. But she didn't even look at me.

'Look after Robin, Charlie,' she said, and she rushed off with Mark.

The two of them together. In a pink Cadillac. Disappearing through a big heart into the dark.

'They've gone,' said Robin.

'Too true,' I said.

'They'll be back soon?' Robin asked.

'How should I know?' I said.

The ride was mostly enclosed, but the first couple's Cadillac suddenly shot through a door overhead and rode through the air in full view of everyone for several seconds. The couple didn't seem to realize. They were kissing.

'Look!' said Robin, giggling.

The first couple disappeared through another dinky door. We waited for the second couple. We waited a long time, and then suddenly they burst through the overhead door. They rode through the air in full view of everyone. They didn't realize either. They were kissing.

'Look!' said Robin, giggling again. And then *he* realized. 'It's Daddy and Jo!'

I didn't say anything. My nose was still hot but the rest of me had turned icy cold.

'But they were kissing. Why were they kissing? They don't kiss,' said Robin, sounding perplexed. He rubbed Birdie's wing against his cheek like a cuddle blanket.

'Looks like they certainly do kiss,' I said. 'So there you go, Robin. Your dad. And my mum. Well, he's not going to be my dad. And she's not going to be *your* mum.'

'I've got a mum,' said Robin.

'Yes, but she doesn't want you any more, does she?' I said.

'Yes, she does,' said Robin uncertainly. 'Daddy said. It's just her new man who doesn't want me.'

'Well, my mum's obviously got herself *her* new man. So she doesn't want me. And your dad's got himself his new lady. So he won't want you either now. Tough, isn't it?'

It made the pain ease just a little if I made Robin

smart too. His face crumpled as he clutched Birdie.
I started to get scared.

      'Hey, don't cry again. I was only joking,' I said.
But we both knew I'd been serious.

SUNDAY

Sunday is meant to be a day of rest. Well, ha ha.
There's no rest as far as I'm concerned. Baby
Freddie wakes up screaming just the same as
always and I have to crawl out of my warm bed
and change his napkins and
give him his bottle, and by
the time he's settled
Louisa comes trailing in
clutching her doll and
Victor leaps up and starts
bouncing on his bed in his
nightgown and I have to
do my best to quieten
them, because it's Sunday.

They have to wear their Sunday best,
even the baby, and by the time I've got all three
laced and buttoned and booted, my chilblains throb
so bad I can barely do up my own clothes. It's my
Sunday best too, though my hideous servant
uniform is nothing to show off about. We all have
to go to church after breakfast. Louisa and Victor
are supposed to sit still in the pew, but of course
they swing their legs and nudge each other and

giggle and I get the blame. If Freddie cries the Master and Mistress glare at me and expect me to stop him — but if he really gets going then I'm allowed to take him out of the church to carry him around outside. When the Vicar is droning on and on I sometimes feel like giving baby Freddie a sly pinch just to escape!

We were never really church folk at home. When Father was alive us children were sent off to Sunday School every week — but I think that was just so Mother and Father had a bit of peace and quiet without us. I liked Sunday School well enough, because you were given a book every year if you attended regularly. I liked singing the hymns too, though the words sometimes made me ponder. 'All things bright and beautiful' is pretty enough, but I do not care for the part where it says God made us high or lowly and each to our estate. In other words, us servants must know our place. Fiddlesticks!

I talked about this with Mrs Angel and Eliza when we were having a cup of cocoa together at the end of the long day. Eliza giggled but Mrs Angel was shocked. She said I was being bad and blasphemous and shooed me out of her kitchen. But Mrs Angel was in a bad mood anyway because she was so tired. Sunday is such a long boring day that everyone wants to eat all the time and she is forever serving meals, her huge roast beef and Yorkshire, with three puddings to follow, and scarcely have they eaten the last morsel than they're ringing the bell for afternoon tea.

The children are bored silly too, because they are not allowed to play with their usual toys. I am supposed to lock away Louisa's favourite doll and bring out her grand Sunday doll with her golden curls and cream silk clothes from France. Louisa admires this doll but does not dare carry her around for fear of mussing her. Victor is not allowed to play any rumbustious boys' games. He is supposed to occupy himself with a suitable Sunday story book, all instruction and no adventures. Victor finds this very dull fare.

It is usually easy to get the children to go to bed on Sundays because they are so eager for it to change to Monday!

I have been tormented these last few Sundays thinking of Mother. Mr Higgins closes the Dog and Duck on a Sunday. I have a terrible feeling that they might be stepping out together. I shall not be able to bear it if Mr Higgins becomes my new father. I did not care for my old father, but I shall care for this one even less.

137

LAW AND ORDER

We were all very quiet in the car going home. Jo and Mark kept giving little quick glances at each other. I couldn't stand it. They both seemed to have forgotten that there were passengers in the back.

I started singing stupid songs as loudly as I could.

'Charlie!' said Jo. 'For heaven's sake, you can't even sing in tune.'

'It's fun to sing in the car,' said Mark. 'Let's all have a sing-song, eh? What about "Ten Green Bottles"? We know that one, don't we, Robin?'

Robin didn't reply. He was scrunched up with Birdie's wing right over his face.

'Are you feeling sick again, Robin?' Jo asked, peering round at him.

No response.

'Is he asleep?' she whispered to me.

'I don't know,' I said, taking a deep breath for my next song.

'Shut up,' said Jo. 'Don't you dare wake him up.'

He wasn't actually asleep. Whenever we were on a brightly lit road I could see the gleam of his eye.

And when I went quiet I could just hear his snuffling above the car engine.

I should have reached out and given him a cuddle. I should have told him that he mustn't worry, of course his dad would still want him. I should have told Mark and Jo that he was crying.

I didn't. Oh, how I wish I had. But I didn't. I stayed hard and hating.

Mark dropped me and Jo off outside our flats.

'Thank you for a fantastic day out,' said Jo, putting her head so close to his that I thought she was going to kiss him again right in front of me. But she straightened out and he started to wind up his window.

'Say thank you, Charlie,' said Jo.

'Thank you,' I said, with absolutely no expression, total Dalek daughter.

'What the hell is the matter with you?' Jo exploded, the moment we were inside our own front door. 'You've been foul the entire day.'

'I'm surprised you noticed. You've only had eyes for one person all day long. Oooh Mark, how lovely, what a treat, gee-whizz how fantastic,' I said, imitating her gushing tone.

She blushed, but she tried to stare me out.

'Grow up a bit,' said Jo. 'You're acting like a toddler whose mum has started to talk to someone else. Surely you don't seriously mind that I've made one nice friend all by myself? You've got hundreds of friends, you always have done, and I've been thrilled you've got such a good independent social life. I've always been useless at making friends. And now for the first time ever I've found someone I get on with, why do you have to make all this fuss?'

'But he's not just a friend, is he?' I said.

'Yes, he is!'

'Don't give me that rubbish. I don't go round snogging my friends.'

'What?'

'You heard. I saw you. On that stupid Stardust ride.'

She went redder than ever, and now she couldn't meet my eyes.

I couldn't stand to look at her either. She looked so stupid and flushed and girlie, like Angela swooning over her beloved rock group or Lisa dithering over Dave Wood. But she was Jo. She was my mother. She was mine.

I didn't say another word to her all evening. We both went to bed early but we didn't sleep. We tossed and turned separately, a great gap in the middle of the bed.

It still seemed like night-time when the phone rang. Jo sat up, looking dazed. 'Have I slept in for work?' she said.

I peered at the alarm clock. 'It's only three o'clock. So who on earth's phoning . . . ?' I said, as I jumped out of bed and ran into the living room. 'Hello?' I said, as I snatched up the phone. 'Hello, who is it?'

'It's Mark here, Charlie.'

I couldn't believe it!

'Can I speak to Jo, please? It's urgent.'

I dropped the receiver as if it were burning me. Jo came rushing into the room.

'Who is it? What's going on?'

'It's only your *friend*,' I said. 'And he says it's *urgent*. Well, would you mind asking him to save his urgent little lovey-dovey messages till it's actually daylight. I'd like to get some sleep before I go to school, if it's all the same to you two lovebirds.'

'Do shut up, Charlie,' said Jo, picking up the receiver. 'Mark? What is it?' She was silent for a few seconds.

I started to do a mime of exaggerated kissing and then pretended to puke. But then I saw the shock on her face and I stopped the pantomime.

'What's happened?' I said.

'It's Robin,' said Jo. 'It's little Robin, he's gone missing.'

The words sizzled in my brain like an electric shock.

'Missing?' I whispered.

Jo was asking Mark heaps of questions, and I could hear the frantic tone of his answers.

'You're *sure* he's not just hiding somewhere? Under his bed? In one of the cupboards? Let me come over and search,' said Jo.

More talk.

'No, I want to come anyway. I'll be with you in ten minutes,' said Jo, and hung up.

She ran to the bathroom. I followed her.

She was on the loo, cleaning her teeth at the same time, shaking her head to wake herself up. She shook it again at me.

'Look, Charlie, I can't take any sneering from you just now. This is nothing to do with Mark and me. It's serious.'

'I know,' I said, biting my knuckle. 'Has Robin really run away?'

'I don't know! Mark woke up and he just popped his head into Robin's room to check up on him – he'd been a bit funny when he put him to bed after the day out – and – and he wasn't there. Mark says he's searched everywhere. I don't see how Robin could have got out the door and run off somewhere, I mean, he's such a timid little thing – oh God, I keep thinking of awful possibilities . . .' Jo was nearly in tears as she rushed round the bathroom and then ran back into the bedroom, pulling on jeans and a jacket over her nightie.

I started yanking on my own clothes too.

'Charlie? Look, you'd better not come. Go back to bed. Maybe you could phone the supermarket later if I'm not back. And you get yourself off to school and—'

'No! I'm coming too! Oh, Jo, something awful will have happened to him, won't it?' I clung to her as if I were a tiny kid myself.

'Hey, hey. We'll find him. He'll be OK,' said Jo, although neither of us believed it. 'Someone will have found him wandering about and—'

'But that's what I'm scared of. What if some really

creepy pervert gets hold of him and—'

'Don't. No. Look, he'll have just wandered down the road – maybe sleepwalking, something like that – and he'll be curled up in a doorway somewhere, perfectly safe, sound asleep.'

'But it's cold out – really cold for a kid like Robin. And if he was just wearing his pyjamas . . .'

'Mark said his school jumper's missing too – and his slippers.'

The thought of Robin setting off in his new too-big school jumper, his pyjamas and his scuffed slippers made me bite my knuckle almost to the bone.

The lights were all on in Mark's flat – and there was a police car outside.

'There! They've found him,' said Jo, taking my hand and hauling us both up the stairs.

But they hadn't found him. Mark had called the police and was telling them over and over again how he'd looked in on Robin's room, and he wasn't in his bed, and he'd gone to the bathroom, he'd gone to the kitchen, gone round and round every room in the house, calling and calling . . . His voice was hoarse now, and his face looked dreadful, pale grey and shiny. He caught hold of Jo but this was different; he was just so desperate to get Robin back safe and she might be able to help.

I might be able to help.

I had to tell them.

I opened my mouth but I couldn't get the words out.

'Don't worry,' said this young policewoman, patting my shoulder. 'We're doing our very best to find him. We've sent out his description and everyone's searching. Children go missing every week – and they nearly always turn up safe and sound.'

'Not kids as little as Robin. It's all my fault,' I said. 'I made him run away. I even gave him that little cake with GET LOST on it.'

'Oh, come on, Charlie – that was silly, yes, but that's got nothing to do with it,' said Jo.

'But I said . . . I said all this hateful stuff . . . when we saw you kissing . . .' I waited.

Mark put his hands on my shoulders. His hands dug right into me. 'What did you say, Charlie?'

'I – I – it was so awful . . .'

'I don't care how awful. You've got to tell us. It might give us some clue where he's gone. I've been running round the streets this past hour, everywhere he goes, down to the shop on the corner, up the road to the park, he's not anywhere – I've looked, I've called – and yet how could he have got further, just wearing his slippers, and he hates going for walks, and he'd never go off willingly without me . . .' Mark's voice cracked.

'I told him you wouldn't want him any more,' I whispered. 'I didn't really mean it, I said I was joking, but – but it was a horrible thing to say to him, I'm so sorry, it made him cry in the car going home

144

and I didn't tell and it's so awful and if anything's happened to him—'

'Nothing will have happened to him,' Jo said, putting her arm round me. We're nearly the same height and yet I seemed to have shrunk and she'd become a great big enveloping mother. 'We'll find him, I promise you, we'll find him.' She was promising Mark too, saying it over and over, trying to convince us.

'What did Robin say when you said all this?' Mark persisted.

'He mentioned his mum. Could he have run away to see her?' I asked.

'She lives in Manchester. How could he possibly . . . ? But I know he's been missing her ever since his last visit. Though he always said he wanted to stay with me when I talked to him about it. Oh, Charlie, *how* could you tell him I didn't want him?' said Mark, tears running down his face.

He wasn't angry with me. Yet. This was far worse. I started to cry too.

'It was a terrible thing to say but you were angry and upset,' said Jo. 'Everyone says terrible things when they feel really bad. Stop it Mark, she's only a kid herself. Can't you see how desperately sorry she is? Don't blame her, blame me. I forced her into that day out. She wasn't ready for it. We've been too close . . .'

I listened to Jo sticking up for me, making all these excuses. It made me feel worse, the worst person in the whole world.

Messages kept crackling over the police radio clipped to the policewoman's shoulder. We froze each time – but it was never to say they'd found him.

'I've got to go and search for him again myself,' said Mark.

'It'll be light soon. I should wait till then,' said the policewoman.

'But Robin's frightened of the dark—'

'He's probably tucked up in a corner somewhere, fast asleep. We've alerted everyone available. They're all searching. We've got the helicopter up too. It's got this special thermal imaging sweep that works even in the dark. The scanner picks up heat from the body—'

'The body?' said Mark, his voice cracking.

'From the person, from your little boy, and it gives off a green image. It's an amazing invention; we've had great success with it.'

But Mark couldn't wait, couldn't stay still, so he went off in one of the patrol cars cruising the area. Jo and I waited in his flat with the policewoman. She made us a cup of tea but when I drank it down it made me feel so sick I only just got to the toilet in time. I splashed cold water on my face afterwards and stared at myself in Mark's bathroom mirror. I felt I was looking at a murderer.

I've never really felt bad about myself before. I could be cheeky, I could be bossy, I could be fierce – but I'd always thought I was one of the good guys. If any little kid at school was getting bullied I'd always charge in and send the bully flying. If

146

anything needed sorting out then all the other kids would turn to me. Everybody liked me. Even the boys.

But now I'd done the meanest thing in the whole world. It didn't matter that I was sorry. Robin had run away and maybe he was going to be lost for ever.

I felt myself folding up so that I was crouching on the bathroom floor, my head banging against the cold edge of the bath. I shut my eyes tight, banging and banging, trying to knock myself backwards, trying to make time tick backwards, so that I could undo and unsay everything. But no matter how I tried I couldn't stop the hands on my watch moving forward, and every minute Robin was still missing.

I heard the whirr of the police helicopter overhead. I wondered if they'd be able to spot Robin staggering along a grass verge, crouching down beside a hedge, curled beneath a tree. He might look up and show Birdie this immense mechanical relation . . . No, if he heard the whirling noise he'd probably be frightened and hide in a doorway, a cardboard box, behind a dustbin, and then he'd never be spotted.

I could see him so vividly in my head, crying, shivering with the cold, clutching Birdie desperately. And then I saw a sinister shadow beside him, someone reaching out and grabbing him, a hand over

147

his mouth so that he couldn't scream . . .

'Charlie? Charlie, let me in.' It was Jo, knocking on the door.

But I needed to stay in there by myself. I scrunched up tight into a ball and I closed my eyes and I mumbled, Please let Robin be all right, Please let Robin be all right, Please let Robin be all right, over and over, until the words concertinaed. I didn't dare stop even for a second – not until I heard the front door bang.

I rushed out of the bathroom. More police. And Mark – holding something small and shabby in his hands.

'Robin?' I whispered.

Mark shook his head. 'I went to the park,' he said, his voice breaking. 'It's still too dark to see properly, but I thought I'd check the pond – I always take him there to feed the ducks. And he's not there – no sign of him – but over by the gate the police officer stood on something. He thought it was a dead bird . . .'

Mark held out the cloth wings and the stained scarlet chest. Birdie.

LAW AND ORDER

Oh my Lord! Baby Freddie is missing and I fear it is all my fault.

I was worn out and near to despairing with all three children. Freddie kept me up half the night wailing and whimpering, then Louisa would *not* wear her proper day dress and insisted on putting on her party silk — and then spilt her porridge all down the front. Victor gave me cheek all morning and when I remonstrated he kicked me hard upon the shin.

I was so cross with my disagreeable and disobedient charges that when we were in the public gardens together I parked the perambulator and stormed off for a few moments by myself, calling all three children as many bad names as I could think of under my breath. When I had calmed down a little I went back again. There was no sound from the perambulator so I assumed baby Freddie had gone to sleep at last. Louisa was over by the pond, feeding the ducks with crusts of stale bread begged from Mrs Angel, while Victor bowled his hoop round and round the pond, singing a vulgar song at the top of his voice.

I told him to hush and begged Louisa to take
care because she was standing right on the edge.
Louisa took no notice and hurled a crust wildly,
lost her balance and toppled over into the water!
The pond is not deep but Louisa went headlong. I
had to hitch up my skirts to wade in and grab her.
Louisa clutched at me wildly, convinced she was
drowning — and over I toppled too.
Victor shrieked with laughter
at the pair of us. I had duck-
weed streaming from my hair
when I struggled out at last,
Louisa under one arm. We
were both sopping wet.
  'Quick! Home at once before
we catch our death of cold,' I
said, shivering, conscious that we
made a right spectacle. I took hold of the
perambulator handle — and peered at the
pillow. No baby Freddie! I pulled back the blankets
frantically, tossing the pillow to one side.
He was gone! I ran desperately
around the perambulator,
wondering if he could possibly
have clambered out by himself.
I wondered if Victor was
playing another prank on me
but one look at his white face
made me see that this time he
wasn't joking.

  Someone had snatched baby Freddie and stolen

him away! I stopped passers-by and asked them if they had seen the little mite. Someone said they'd seen an infant in the arms of some scoundrelly looking creature and I started shrieking. I ran home with Victor and Louisa, pushing the empty perambulator. I had to tell the Mistress. I could scarce get the words out. She had a fit of the vapours at the terrible news and Eliza had to fetch the smelling bottle. Mrs Angel ran down the road to find her policeman friend and he took all the particulars. He swears he will search every thieves' den in the town, for he thinks Freddie has been stolen to be held to ransom. He is going to write to the police station in the neighbouring district, and a piece will be put in the *Police Gazette.*

He said that once he catches the varmint responsible he will have him publicly flogged and if he has harmed the baby then he will hang by the neck until he is dead.

Oh my Lord, I am so scared. If only I hadn't stormed off like that. If only I had kept a watch on the perambulator all the time! If only, if only, if only!

SICKNESS

'They'll find him,' Jo kept saying. 'He'll be in the park. Or nearby. They'll find him when it's light. He'll have just fallen asleep now, Mark, that's all.'

'The helicopter hasn't tracked him down. And we've looked everywhere. All over the park,' said Mark, hugging Birdie to his chest. 'We called and called. They're still there now, calling. If he was asleep he'd wake up and hear. He could be in the pond – they're going to dredge it. He could be lying in a ditch somewhere—'

'Don't think like that, Sir. There's no reason to think the worst,' said the policewoman. 'I've been with parents so many times, and they've been going through agonies like this but it's always turned out well in the end—'

'That's right, Mark. We've got to be positive,' said Jo, putting her arm round him. She held her other arm out to me. 'Come here, Charlie.'

But I couldn't go. I felt too ashamed. Police came, police went. The phone rang but it was Mark's ex-wife, ringing from an all-night motorway café. She was on her way here with her new man, desperate to know if there was any further news. The policewoman made more tea, endless cups, although no-one took more than a few sips of each fresh brew. Someone switched on the radio at six and tuned it into the local station.

'*A five-year-old boy is missing from his home in Newcombe Way,*' said a voice. '*Little Robin West is small and slight, dark hair, dark eyes, believed to be wearing nightclothes and a grey sweater . . .*'

It made it all so horribly real hearing Robin's name on the radio. Everyone's head jerked at the sound.

More news bulletins kept tuning into my head. Imaginary ones with terrible news. I put my hands over my ears, but I couldn't block out the sound of my own thoughts.

Then the police radio crackled again, and the policewoman answered it.

'You're sure? He's OK?'

We all stared, hardly daring to hope.

'Robin?' said Mark, springing up.

'Yes, I think it is!' said the policewoman. 'Small boy, dark hair, found at the railway station. He'd crawled behind a whole pile of parcels awaiting delivery, so no-one spotted him at first.'

'He's all right?' said Mark, tears pouring down his face.

'I think so, Sir – but freezing cold, so they're taking him straight to the hospital. We'll take you there right away.'

'We have to go too,' said Jo, pulling me up.

I didn't dare believe it until we got to the hospital. I kept thinking it would be some other little boy – it couldn't be Robin because I was so sure he was lost for ever now, and that it was all my fault, and that I would hate myself for the rest of my life.

Jo knew, and held my hand very tight all the way there, and when Mark ran forward at the hospital Jo elbowed our way through too.

'She has to see him, just for a few seconds,' she said when nurses tried to catch hold of us.

There was something so commanding in her voice that they let us through. There were more nurses at a bed, a doctor with a stethoscope, a policeman, all circling a narrow bed containing a small tinfoil parcel like a chicken ready to be roasted for Sunday dinner. A flushed face peered out of one end, a smaller bird than a chicken. A Robin.

'Oh, Robin!' I whispered. 'It really is you!'

He didn't hear me. He was too busy blinking up at Mark.

'Daddy!' he said. 'What are you doing here?'

'What are *you* doing here, you silly sausage?' said Mark, and he bent and kissed the tiny bit of Robin that was exposed. 'Oh, Robin, you've led us a merry dance! What did you run away for? We've been so scared.'

'I was scared too. I wanted Mummy—'

'Mummy's coming. She'll be here soon. And you can see her for as long as you like. But Robin, you do know we *both* love you and want you. You're the most important little guy in my life. I was so frightened when I found your bed empty.'

'I had a nasty dream and I wanted Mummy so I got Birdie and we thought we'd go and see her.'

'In Manchester? But Robin, how could you possibly think you could walk to Manchester?' said Mark.

'You get the train. You took me once. We went through the park to the station so that's what we did, Birdie and me, but when we went past the pond the ducks woke up and quacked at us and scared us and then . . . and then . . .' Robin burst into tears.

'You dropped Birdie – but look, Robin, look!' said Mark, producing Birdie, who flew down onto Robin's chest, one wing touching his cheek. 'Birdie's got more sense than you, Robin. He flew home to Daddy.'

I wanted to talk to Robin myself, to tell him how sorry I was.

'Not now,' said Jo, pulling me away. 'He just needs Mark. And we don't want to be here when his mother comes. We'll go home.'

It seemed extraordinary to be back at our flat, having breakfast at the usual time. Whole weeks seemed to have gone by since yesterday.

'You ought really to go back to bed,' said Jo. 'You look exhausted.'

I was far too wound up to sleep. 'I still can't believe he's safe!' I said.

'I said he would be!' said Jo, hugging me.

'Don't, Jo. You've been so nice to me. When I was so wicked.'

'But you didn't mean it.'

'I should still be terribly punished.'

'Well, what do you want me to do? Whip you? Shut you up in a cupboard for a week? Shave all your lovely long hair off and paint you purple?'

'I mean it, Jo. I feel . . . bad. Robin *will* be all right now, won't he?'

'Yes, of course. Once they've got him all warmed up and checked over then I'm sure he'll be able to go home.'

'And can we go round and see him straight away?'

'Well, not if his mother's there too. I don't want to look as if I'm butting in. And maybe this might bring them back together again as a family . . .'

I didn't dare ask her if she'd mind terribly.

Jo went off to the supermarket to explain why she was so late – and I went to school.

Lisa and Angela came charging up to me the minute I set foot in the classroom.

'Hey, Charlie! Did you hear on the radio? That little boy who went missing, Robin. Isn't he the one your mum looks after?'

So I had to say yes, and then when I told them we'd been with Robin's dad half the night and that I'd actually seen Robin in the hospital they asked me dozens of questions, and practically all the class

156

gathered round wanting to hear. So I had to turn it into a proper story and spin it out a bit while they all gasped and exclaimed. They didn't even quieten down when Miss Beckworth swept into the room and told everyone to go to their seats.

'Miss Beckworth, Charlie's practically headline news, she helped find that little boy. Tell Miss Beckworth, Charlie!'

So I told the story all over again, though I was starting to tire of the whole tale. It didn't seem right that even Miss Beckworth seemed mildly impressed. But then she asked the one question I was dreading. Trust her.

'Why did the little boy run away, I wonder?'

I just shrugged and backed away to my desk, sharpish.

Jamie stared at me, looking a little puzzled. 'I love the way you tell things, Charlie. Making it ever so exciting and funny,' he said.

I made little slurpy noises with my lips, to show I thought he was sucking up to me.

'But did it all really happen?' Jamie persisted.

'Yes! What do you think I am, some kind of nutter with a compulsion to tell blatant lies to everyone?'

'But how come your mum looks after this little boy? I thought you said she was a lecturer, like mine?'

I took a deep breath, thinking hard. A blatant lie indeed. Well, call it an elaborate evasion. It was time for another.

'She lost that job, right? So for the moment she ... she teaches little Robin.'

I had to tell my story all over again at playtime to kids in different classes, and they went off and told other kids, so that by dinner time it was all over the school. There were many different versions by this time. Some assumed that my mum and Robin's dad were already a definite item, which infuriated me.

HERO!

Others gave me an even more prominent role in the story, so that I'd gone out in the early morning and tracked Robin through the park to the station all by myself. It was starting to turn into a story about how I'd saved little Robin's life.

It was a relief when school was over at last. I went rushing straight home, wondering if Jo would be round at Mark's place with Robin.

But she was at home, looking tired out herself, pulling fluff out of her bunny jumper, pick pick pick.

'Is Mark's ex-wife round at his place then?' I asked delicately.

'I think she's at the hospital. With Mark,' said Jo.

'What? Is Robin still there then?' I paused. 'He is OK, isn't he?'

Jo's fingers fidgeted down the sleeve of her fluffy jumper. 'Well, I'm sure he's going to be OK, yes, but ...'

'But what? Tell me!'

'I don't really know much. Mark only had ten pence for the phone. He just said that the doctor was a bit worried about Robin's chest—'

'His chest?'

'Apparently he's always been slightly asthmatic, and he did get very chilled, so now he's got a touch of pneumonia.'

'Pneumonia! People die of pneumonia!'

'Now calm down, Charlie. There's no need to get yourself all worked up. I promise Robin's not going to die—'

'You promised he'd be as right as rain, out of hospital as soon as they'd got him warmed up.'

'Well, he *will* be as right as rain. They'll just need to give him some antibiotics.'

'And people always get completely better after pneumonia if they take antibiotics?'

'Well, nearly always. How do I know anyway?'

'Let's go and see him now.'

'I shouldn't imagine he can have too many visitors. He'll need to be kept quiet. He's got his dad – and his mum.' Jo's jumper was going to be picked bald quite soon.

'Couldn't we go to the hospital just to ask if we could see him for two minutes?' I said.

'No, we can't just keep pushing in,' said Jo.

I kept going on at her. I can always wear her down. I had to see Robin again. I hadn't been able to talk to him when he was trussed up in tinfoil like a tiny turkey. I had to tell him something.

159

But I still didn't get a chance. We found our way to the children's ward and it was still visiting time so we walked the long length of the polished floor, looking for Robin. There was no sign of him.

We walked back again, pausing at every bed. There was one empty one and I suddenly took Jo's hand.

'Can I help you?' said a nurse, hurrying past.

'We're looking for Robin West,' said Jo anxiously. 'He's the little boy who was lost.'

'Yes, I know. He's in the side ward up at the end – but I'm not sure he should have any more visitors,' said the nurse.

'There, Charlie,' said Jo. 'I told you.'

'Couldn't we just put our heads round the door to say hello?' I pleaded.

'I suppose you can take a quick peep, if you promise to be quiet,' said the nurse.

'As a mouse,' I said.

When we got near the side ward we walked on tiptoe, though the polish made our shoes squeak like real mice. We were still hand in hand. Our clasp was clammy.

I put my head round the door first. There was Mark, sitting right by the bed, his head in his hands. A pretty blonde woman with a pinched face was wiping her red eyes. And there was Robin lying very still in bed, his face milky white, his eyes closed. Birdie was on his chest, wings spread.

'He's dead!' I burst out, forgetting all about my promise to be quiet.

Robin stirred and whimpered.

'Who on earth . . . ?' said the blonde woman, glaring at me.

'What do you want, Charlie?' said Mark, standing up. His grey face was going patchy red with anger. 'Haven't you done enough?'

'I just wanted to say . . . I'm sorry,' I said.

'Oh, that makes all the difference in the world, does it?' said Mark.

Jo was tugging at me to get me to go. 'We shouldn't have come. We were both just so worried about Robin,' she muttered. 'Come *on*, Charlie.'

'He is going to get better, isn't he?' I said desperately.

Mark ignored me but touched Jo on the shoulder to reassure her. The blonde woman tightened her eyebrows.

'He's still got a high temperature but they're pumping him full of antibiotics and they keep saying he'll be fine,' he said. Then his eyes swivelled to me. 'No thanks to you.'

I let Jo tug me out of the doorway and out of the ward. We had to wait a long while for a bus outside the hospital and then it was a twenty-minute walk home. Jo kept talking to me but I hardly said anything.

She thought it was because I was scared of crying

161

in public. When we got home at last she put her arms round me and said, 'Right, you can let it all out now. Have a really good cry and then you'll feel better.'

I did cry a bit. Jo did too. I don't know whether she felt better. I didn't.

I felt really bad at school the next day. Angela and Lisa still kept on about Robin, asking if I'd seen him and how he was, wanting me to tell them all about it.

'Look, I don't really want to talk about Robin,' I said.

'What are you on about? You did nothing *but* talk about Robin yesterday,' said Lisa.

'OK, OK. That was yesterday. This is today, right? Let's talk about something *else*,' I said.

Angela immediately started burbling about the birthsigns of her beloveds and I groaned and pretended to gag.

'There's no need to take that attitude,' said Angela, hurt. 'You told me to talk about something else, so I did. There's no pleasing you sometimes, Charlie.'

'Hey, my dad says he's still taking us to the Red River Theme Park for my birthday,' said Lisa. 'Which rides are the best, Charlie? Come on, you didn't get a chance to tell us yesterday.'

'No!' I said fiercely.

'You can be a right pain sometimes, Charlie,' said Lisa huffily. 'There's me inviting you out on my birthday treat and yet you just shout at me.'

'Yeah, I can't stick it when you throw a moody like this,' said Angela. 'You think you can treat us like dirt, Charlie Enright, but we might just start to get fed up with it. Isn't that right, Lisa?'

'You bet,' said Lisa. 'Come on, Angela.'

They walked off across the playground arm in arm. I was left all by myself.

I decided I didn't care a bit. There were lots of other girls desperate to be my friend. Or even boys. Like Jamie.

I went and found him in his usual place, head deep in a book. Still *Tess of the d'Urbervilles*, but he'd nearly finished it, even though it's hundreds and hundreds of pages long.

'You'll go cross-eyed reading so much,' I said, flopping down beside him. 'Are you really enjoying that?'

'It's great,' said Jamie. 'Here, Tess murders this guy at the end, the one who had his wicked way with her – Alec.'

'The one she had the baby with?' I said. I tried to remember the film, but I just had this hazy picture of pretty girls in white frocks doing a dance, and afterwards Jo and I had done our own dance in our white nighties. 'Did Tess have a daughter or a son?'

'A little boy.'

'So what happens to him? I don't think there was a little boy in the film.'

'No, he dies when he's a baby.'

'What of?'

'I don't know. I don't think it says.'

'Babies don't just *die*.'

'They did then. Especially little puny ones. They just need to get a little cold and then it develops into pneumonia or something—'

'Shut up!' I shouted.

Jamie jumped. 'What's up?' he said. 'Hey, Charlie – where are you going?'

I didn't know where I was going. I wanted to get away from him, away from Lisa and Angela, away from the whole school . . .

I made for the gate, deciding to make a dash for it and bunk off school for the afternoon. But Miss Beckworth was on playground duty and her eagle eyes were beady-bright.

'Charlotte Enright! Where on earth do you think you're going, young lady?' she called.

I was so desperate I kept on running but I collided with a bunch of little kids coming back into school after going home for dinner. I tripped as I dodged them and fell flat.

I heard them squealing excitedly. Ominous footsteps paused by my side. I didn't try to get up. I just lay where I was – and cried.

'Out of the way, children. There's no need to gawp. Off you go. Shoo!' said Miss Beckworth. She seemed to be bending down beside me. 'Charlotte?'

I howled harder.

'I need to know if you've really hurt yourself badly and need medical attention,' said Miss Beckworth. 'Can you try and sit up so we can examine the damage?'

So I had to sit up, snivelling and snorting. I'd cut my knee and grazed the other, but it was nothing much. Certainly nothing to cry about. Though I was spouting like a fountain.

Some other kids were coming nearer, eyes popping at the sight of Charlie Enright bawling her eyes out.

'Will you go *away*, please?' Miss Beckworth said briskly. 'Charlotte, you'd better come with me.'

She put her hand under my armpits and got me to my feet. She walked me across the playground, shielding me from the stares. She took me right into school and sat me down in the empty classroom.

'There.' She looked at me, and felt up her sleeve for a tissue. 'Use this.'

I blew and mopped.

'That's better. Now. What's the matter?'

'I'm not crying because I fell over,' I said.

'I realize that.'

'And I'm not crying because I shouted at Jamie. Though I feel bad about that.'

'I expect Jamie's used to your shouting at him,' said Miss Beckworth drily.

'And I shouted at Lisa and Angela too and I think they've broken friends with me, but I'm not crying about that either,' I said.

'So . . . what are you crying about?'

I said nothing.

'The little boy who was lost?'

I nodded. 'He's ill. He's got pneumonia. Everyone says he's going to be all right, but I'm so scared that maybe . . .' I cried harder.

'Now, calm down, Charlotte. I haven't got any more tissues! You mustn't worry. Look, I've had pneumonia myself and I recovered perfectly. I know you're obviously very fond of this little boy—'

'No, I'm not! I've been horrid to him. *That's* why I'm crying. You think I'm being all kind and concerned but it's because I've been so bad.'

'Oh dear,' said Miss Beckworth. 'Go on. I think I'm pretty shockproof after twenty-five years of teaching. So tell me.'

So I did. All of it. And stuff about Jo and me from way back. Stuff I'd never dream of telling anyone – let alone *Miss Beckworth*.

She listened to it all – and then she put her arm round me and let me cry on her shoulder even though I was all slurpy and snotty.

'I know you think you're all-powerful, but the little boy didn't run away *just* because of you,' said Miss Beckworth. 'You're only a little part of all this. You were a bit silly and spiteful but you're truly sorry now – and you certainly didn't mean any of this to happen. I'm sure the little boy will get better.'

'You're really sure?' I said, sniffing. 'Because you're never wrong about anything, are you?'

166

'That's right!' said Miss Beckworth. 'Now, you'd better run along and wash that poor old face. Try to cheer up, Charlie.'

It wasn't until I was right along in the girls' cloak-rooms that I realized. Miss Beckworth had called me *Charlie*!

SICKNESS

He's been found! I can scarcely believe it. Little
Freddie is back with us — though we are all still so
worried about the poor lamb because he is sick.

He wasn't taken by thieves and robbers. It was
a woman half-demented because all her own
babies had died. She watched us in the public
gardens, she admired Freddie's chubby cheeks and
golden curls — and when Louisa fell in the pond
and I rushed in after her this woman snatched our
Freddie and made off with him.

She was all set to make him her child, but her
brain was so addled she scarcely fed our poor
little boy and left his napkin unchanged. She
covered him with just one thin sheet at night and
of course the poor child caught a chill. She took
fright as he grew dangerously sick and eventually she wrapped him in her cloak and left
him on the doorstep of the
foundling hospital. (She was
observed and followed, and is
now in police custody.)

The Master and Mistress were sent
for when Freddie was found and great was their

rejoicing – but their joy turned to terror when they saw the state of their poor darling. They took him home and we put him straight to bed and called the doctor. He listened to Freddie's rasping breathing and felt his fevered brow.

'There is nothing I can do,' he said sorrowfully. 'Keep him warm, feed him sugared water, and let us hope the Good Lord sees fit to spare him.'

The Mistress and I have been taking turns to nurse him. For once we are not like Mistress and servant at all. We are more like sisters, united in our desire for Freddie to recover. I feel as much for Freddie now as little Ada–May at home.

Victor and Louisa are being as good as gold. Eliza is looking after them, while I nurse Freddie. Mrs Angel is forever bringing him bowls of nourishing broth but the poor mite is too poorly to even suck the spoon.

Oh, please let him be saved!

SEASIDE

We were back to Charlotte the next day. We had English first lesson, one of those boring writing exercises – a formal letter of apology. It seemed a perfect opportunity to make things up with Lisa and Angela. (I didn't need to go to letter-writing lengths with Jamie as I was sitting right beside him. I could just give him a nudge and mumble, 'Sorry I yelled at you to shut up. You can tell me to shut up some time if you want.' Jamie blinked at me. 'I'd have to make sure you were in a good mood first!' he said – displaying his famous intelligence.)

Anyway, I got cracking with my apology letter. I think I did it beautifully, in my very best hand-writing, no blotches, no smears. I put my address at the right-hand corner, I remembered the date, I flaunted an amazingly varied vocabulary, I didn't make a single spelling mistake, I signed off appropriately, and I even personally decorated my piece of paper. You look:

My Desk
Miss Beckworth's Class
Avondale Junior School

Truly Terrible Tuesday

Dear Lisa and Angela,
  Do not rip this letter up in disgust when you see it's from the appalling, beastly, crosspatch, dolthead, egotistic, foul, gross, horrible, irritating, jealous, knavish, loathsome, mangy, nerve-wracking, odious, presumptuous, quarrelsome, ratty, spoilt, terrible, unkind, verminous, wicked, X-rated, yucky, zero
    called Charlotte Alice Katherine Enright

UTTERLY FOUL

        (commonly known as Charlie), who used to
        be your friend. No wonder you both broke
        friends with me! I have been Utterly Foul
        (though with just cause seeing as I've had
        Terrible Things on my Mind) but that is no
        excuse to be hateful to you two, who are the
dearest sweetest kindest friends any girl could
ever wish for. And if I had a wish it would
be this: Please will you make friends with
me again?

wish wish wish wish wish

  Yours utterly sincerely — and with
lots of luv and XXXXXXXX
  Charlie

Jamie read my letter over my shoulder (I let him because I was trying so hard to be a new sweet person) and he cracked up laughing.

'That's a merry sound, James – but a little inappropriate in a classroom,' said Miss Beckworth. 'Please tell me why you're laughing.'

Jamie had long since stopped laughing. He had gone red and stammery. 'I – I was just clearing my throat, Miss Beckworth,' he said.

'I not only have all-seeing eyes, James. I also have all-hearing ears. You were not clearing your throat. You were laughing. Why?'

Jamie shifted desperately on his chair. He's so weird, he gets so worried the rare times he gets told off. I expected him to blurt out that he'd laughed because of my letter but he kept his lip buttoned to try to keep me out of trouble. Which was sweet of him, but a total waste of time.

Miss Beckworth was looking at me, eyebrows raised, one arm extended. 'Bring me that piece of paper, Charlotte. How dare you mess around instead of getting on with your set written work.'

'It *is* my written work, Miss Beckworth,' I said, taking it out to her.

She read my letter. For one second her lips twitched – and I thought I was going to be OK. No such luck.

'This is *not* a formal letter of apology, Charlotte,' said Miss Beckworth.

'It *is* – sort of,' I insisted unwisely. 'You know what I'm like, Miss Beckworth. I always have to do things my way.'

'I appreciate that, Charlotte. There is just one small point you seem to have missed. This is my class, not yours. In my class we do things *my* way. And you will do me a proper sensible sticking-to-the-rules formal letter of apology now, and you will write out another *five* formal letters of apology, all different, at home tonight. That might make you reflect a little and learn that it makes more sense to do things my way right from the start.'

That was the most amazingly atrocious punishment of all time – especially as I wanted to do something extremely important and very time-consuming that evening. But even I realized it would be unwise to argue further. It seemed utterly unbelievable that such a cruel unbending beastly teacher could have let me cry all over her jumper just yesterday, but there you go.

The one weeny good thing was that she gave me my original letter back, so I could give it to Angela and Lisa at playtime. They laughed too. Lots. And we're best friends all over again, so at least that's something.

I got started on my five foul letters the minute I got home. It took me ages but I knew it would be foolish to fudge them. I actually wrote a sixth letter, just a little one.

Dear Miss Beckworth,

This is partly yet another formal letter of apology. I am sorry I mess around at everything. I will truly try to do things your way. Though it will be very very difficult.

This is also an informal letter of thanks. Thank

you for letting me say all that stupid stuff on Monday. Sorry I used up your tissues! And you were right, because Robin is lots better!

Yours sincerely,
Charlotte

Mark might have made it plain that he wanted nothing to do with me, but he phoned Jo to tell her that Robin's temperature had gone down, his chest was clear, and the antibiotics were obviously doing their job well.

'So is Robin properly awake now, sitting up and able to look at things?' I asked.

'Yes, but I'm not taking you to the hospital again, no matter what you say,' said Jo.

'It's OK. I can see we can't go. Mark really hates me now, doesn't he?' I said.

'No, of course he doesn't. He's just still terribly wound up and anxious over Robin,' said Jo.

'And he blames me.'

'He wasn't thinking straight.'

'Look, *I* blame me. But it's just sort of weird. Being hated by someone.'

'He doesn't hate you, I keep saying that. And anyway, it doesn't even matter if he does because you don't have to see him ever again. He probably won't want me to work for him any more, let alone . . .' Jo's voice tailed away. She looked so miserable I couldn't bear it.

'Jo? I'm sorry I've mucked things up for you and him,' I mumbled.

174

Jo gave me a push. 'What rubbish! You're not the slightest bit sorry about that, Charlie! You did your level best to spoil things right from the start. And I don't know why you're carrying on about Mark not liking you, because you made it amazingly plain that you hated him.'

'Yes, I know. I couldn't stand it when he smarmed all over me, and kept trying to take my side. But now . . . I still don't like him but I want him to like me.'

'That's just typical of you, you spoilt brat,' said Jo. 'Have you finished all your letters? Shall we go to bed and watch telly for a bit?'

'*You're* the one that spoilt me! Not that I blame you, of course. Seeing as I'm so chock full of charm.'

'Ha! Come on, I can't be too late. I daren't mess them about at the supermarket after missing my Monday shift.'

'I want to do a bit of drawing first. You go. I promise I won't wake you if you go to sleep first, I'll creep in ever so quietly.'

I sat up for hours doing my drawing. I drew a bed in the middle of the page, with a pale little boy and a tiny toy bird propped up on the pillows. Then in all the rest of the space I did an immense flock of birds come to wish Robin and Birdie better. I did great eagles and albatrosses swooping round the ceiling, parrots and cockatoos and canaries singing silly songs, soft doves fanning him with their feathers, lovebirds billing and cooing above his head, tiny wrens whizzing every which way while swallows

flitted in strict formation, ostriches and emus picking their way cautiously across the polished floor, little fluffy chicks cheeping in clumps, proud peacocks spreading their tails as screens around the bed.

I coloured it all in as carefully as I could, until my

eyes watered and my hand ached. But it was done at long last – and I just hoped Robin would like it.

Jo came rushing in to tell me *she* liked it at half past five in the morning.

'Hey! I didn't wake you up last night,' I grumbled under the covers. 'Can you stick it in an envelope and post it to Robin at the hospital?'

Jo said she would – but when I got home from school that day she told me she'd taken it to the hospital herself.

'It would have spoilt it, folding it all up to fit into an envelope. So I took it to the hospital after I'd been to the Rosens'. I was just going to give it to one of the nurses but then I bumped into Mark quite by chance . . .'

'Oh yeah!'

'What are you looking at me like that for? Anyway, he seemed quite happy about me having a peep at Robin, and he's doing wonderfully. They think he can come out of hospital by the end of the week. And I showed him your picture and he just loves it, Charlie; he spent ages and ages looking at all the different birds and now he's got it pinned up on the wall beside his bed. Mark was so pleased. He looks a bit better himself now that Robin's recovering. He's taken the next week off his work too, and he's talking about taking Robin to the seaside.'

'With Robin's mum?'

'Ah. No. She's had to go back to Manchester – when she knew Robin was going to be all right.'

'Has that upset him?'

'Well. He obviously misses his mother a great deal, but Mark was always the one who looked after him most even when they were together.'

'She looked a right cow to me,' I said.

'Charlie!' said Jo. But she looked pleased.

'What about Mark? Does he miss her too?'

'Well . . . He doesn't seem to, no. He said things were never very good between them, and they had all these rows—'

'Yeah, listen and proceed cautiously, Josephine! *That's* what marriage is all about. Rows,' I said, wagging my finger at her. 'Don't you dare think of ever getting married, right?'

I did another picture for Robin that night. This time I drew him in a warm red woolly jumper with a pair of massive feathery wings sticking out the back, brown to match his trousers, real robin colours, and he and Birdie were flying over the sea with a flock of seagulls, and they all had sticks of rock or candy-floss

or portions of fish and chips in their beaks and way down below there was a beach and everyone was waving and pointing and smiling up at them.

Jo took it in to Robin at the hospital. This time I got my own picture back. It was a portrait of me. Well, it had my name on it in very wobbly letters. My hair was an orange scribble right down past my knees. My eyes were crossed. My arms stuck straight out of my neck. My legs were mostly hidden beneath a triangle of green frock, but my feet were vast and stuck out sideways.

'Hmmm,' I said. 'Is this supposed to be flattering?'

'He tried ever so hard,' said Jo. 'This was his third attempt.'

'What's this pointy thing sticking in me? A dagger? Did Mark add that?'

'It's an arrow, pointing to you, to show you're Charlie. And Mark doesn't want to stick any daggers in you, you daft girl. In fact he wants you to come to the hospital tomorrow to see Robin.'

'Oh, wow, His Lordship has given his orders, eh?' I said.

'Charlie?' said Jo. 'Oh, don't be like that.'

'Don't look so worried. I'll go. To see Robin.'

'Are you going to do him another picture?'

'How about one he can eat?'

I wanted to make him a proper robin cake in the shape of a bird, but I couldn't work out how to do it, and the wing tips and little claws would be far too fiddly and break off. So in the end I made two ordinary round sponges and sandwiched them together with lots of butter cream and jam and then I made up this super brown butter icing with a bit of cocoa powder and smeared it over most of the cake, doing an extra feathery layer each side for wings, and then I stuck on two brown smarties for eyes and a yellow one for the beak, and I filled in the gap with new bright-red butter icing.

It all took much longer than I'd thought, and the robin cake still didn't look quite right.

'It's wonderful!' said Jo.

'No, it looks like the robin's been severely squashed,' I said, sighing.

I really wanted to stay up all night and try again, but I'd used up all the eggs and icing sugar and practically half our housekeeping money, so I couldn't.

I kept worrying about the stupid cake the next day at school. Or maybe I was worrying about going to the hospital. Or something.

I took my time going home from school.

'Come on, what kept you?' said Jo. 'We won't get there in time for Robin's tea at this rate.'

'I don't feel like trailing all the way over there,' I said. 'You go.'

'After you've made Robin the fantastic cake?'

'It's a stupid cake. But you can take it if you think he'd really like it.'

'You're the one that's being stupid. Dump your schoolbag, find your jacket, and let's get cracking,' said Jo. Firmly.

So I went to the hospital clutching my cake in a tin. Mark didn't smile at me, but he nodded. Robin put his head on one side shyly, but he had this great big grin on his face.

'It's *Charlie!*' he whispered – as if I were someone important.

I don't like little kids much. Especially little boys. But somehow I dumped my cake tin and put my arms round Robin and gave him a great big hug. He'd always been a skinny little thing but now he felt like one of those little glass animals that snap off an arm or a leg when you just look at them. I tried not to hug him too hard in case I hurt him. Then I had to hug Birdie too. His general appearance hadn't been improved by Robin's recent adventures. I didn't really enjoy having this filthy piece of cloth rubbed round my face, but I didn't complain.

My cake had got a bit bashed about inside the tin, but it was still just about recognizable as a robin. The real Robin didn't want to cut it at first, but I made Birdie pretend to be starving hungry and nibble a corner of the cake, so Robin gave in.

It wasn't a work of art *ornithologically* (ha!) but it certainly tasted good. Robin had a great big slice. So did Mark and Jo and two nurses and a couple of kids in the main ward that Robin had made friends with. I had a great big slice as well. Two, actually, just to check it tasted good all the way round.

'It's a lovely cake,' said Mark, giving me another

nod. Then he smiled at Jo. 'I expect you helped Charlie with it?'

I spluttered. 'Jo can't even make *toast*!'

I felt like clouting him with the cake tin. But I didn't. I sensed our relationship was still dead precarious. I still couldn't stick him. I didn't ever want to make friends with him. But I did want to be friends with Robin.

Mark took him to the seaside the next week. Bournemouth. I'd never been there.

'I have,' said Jo. 'Your grandma and grandpa used to take me there on holiday when I was little. In a big white hotel and they played tennis all day and whist in the evening and I just mooched about, too shy and stupid to make friends with any of the other kids.'

'Aaaaah!' I said, teasing her. 'Don't worry, *I'll* play with you next time we go to the seaside.'

'We could go to Bournemouth on Saturday,' said Jo, trying to sound casual. 'Meet up with Robin and Mark. Mark phoned and suggested it.'

Jo still had to do her supermarket shift early Saturday morning, but I met her at eight o'clock and we went straight to the station and set off for Bournemouth. Robin and Mark met us off the train. Robin looked a bit bigger and bouncier out of bed, though he was so well wrapped up against the sea breeze that he could barely move. Birdie's appearance had deteriorated even more because he'd dived into the sea by mistake when Robin was paddling in wellie boots – but at least he'd had a good wash.

It was a bit nippy for the beach but we walked right along the sands and I laboured long and hard making a sandcastle for Robin. He twittered beside me and Jo and Mark billed and cooed in the background. I was beginning to think I'd maybe done enough hard labour and that it was time I was let off for good behaviour – but I perked up a little when Mark bought us all ice creams.

It was far too cold to go swimming in the sea, of course, but we went to the Leisure Pool instead. Birdie took a nap in a locker while Robin splashed around happily with me. Robin still looked a bit too thin stripped to his bathing costume but he was very perky. Mark looked a right berk in his trunks. I practically fell about laughing.

We spent ages drying every tiny bit of Robin afterwards and wrapping him back in his one hundred and one layers and then we had hot chocolate to make sure he was well and truly warmed up before going out into the wind.

We went on the pier and Mark spent a small fortune on the cuddly-toy cranes. He's useless at them . . . but *eventually* he won a lop-sided parrot for

183

Robin and a simpering blue
bunny for Jo. And then he got this
hideous bug-eyed troll with long
orange hair – and gave it to me.

I wasn't particularly charmed with that little
seaside souvenir. But I tell you what I *did* get.
There's an amazing museum place in Bournemouth
called the Russell-Coates Gallery. It's this big
Victorian house and it's stuffed full of everything
Victorian and I went round and round peering at
everything, pretending I'd really stepped back
into the past. No nurseries, though – my
Lottie wouldn't have had a job.

Robin needed to have a wee so I
took him into this lavatory – and it was
a genuine Victorian one, with a special
picture down the pan and a great big
wooden seat. I tried it out too.

I hoped I'd be able to buy a postcard of it, but no
such luck. I bought lots of other postcards, though.
Not for Lottie's diary. It had become obvious to me
that Miss Beckworth was not going to approve of
my project. It was very much *my* way, not hers. And
yet there was no way I was going to change it now.
So I decided if I couldn't win a prize for best
Victorian project then I might as well make sure
that Jamie did. I bought all the postcards for him.

SEASIDE

Dear little Freddie pulled through! One night his fever rose alarmingly and he didn't know any of us and we all really felt this was the end — but towards dawn he quietened and grew calm and suddenly opened his eyes and said 'Mamma' as clear as anything. He took a long drink and then settled down into a peaceful sleep. He woke at lunchtime almost his old self, though his sweet curls were all in a tangle and his face pale and drawn. He lapped up all his broth and made it plain that he wanted more.

The Mistress cried, Mrs Angel cried, Eliza cried — and oh how I cried too! We were all so tired and strung out watching over little Freddie that the  Master decided to take a week away from his business and hire rooms for us all at the seaside as soon as Freddie was fit to travel.

We went on the steam train, an amazing adventure! Victor was beside himself with glee, asking questions nineteen to the dozen — and Louisa insisted on sticking her head out of the

window and got
herself covered
in sooty smuts.

It was dark
when we arrived at long last and there was such
a to—do getting the children to bed and all our
belongings unpacked that I simply crawled into my
own bed and fell fast asleep while Eliza and Mrs
Angel were still joshing and giggling (we three
share a room in the seaside lodgings and it is very
companionable). But I awoke early. I looked in on
Freddie but he was still fast asleep, and there
wasn't a peep from Louisa or Victor either. So I
wrapped myself in my cloak and ran down to see
the sea.

I could not believe it. I knew it would be a very
large stretch of water, but I'd pictured it like the
river at home. I had no idea it would shimmer as
far as the eye could see. And it moved so, wave
after wave rolling over and over.

It was very cold in the early morning air but I
tore my boots and stockings off and paddled in
the shallows just to say I had done it! A fat
old woman told me I could use one of
her bathing machines if I cared to,
but I was happy enough just to let
the water whirl about my ankles.
My feet were blue with cold all
morning but I didn't care.

Then, when I took the three
children to the beach later that

morning there was an ice-cream man selling
hokey-pokey for a penny a lump, even though it
was the winter season. I had three pennies so I
bought one for Louisa, one for Victor, and one for
Freddie and me to share.

My first ice cream! This time my lips
turned blue but I licked them warm again.

I still cannot say I enjoy being a
servant — but it has its compensations!

CHRISTMAS

Jamie's Victorian project *did* win. Well, it was obvious it was going to. It was easy-peasy, simple-pimple to work it out. Though my postcards from Bournemouth certainly helped. They made Jamie's project much thicker and the pages clicked enticingly as you turned each page. These postcard pages were so bright and glossy that Miss Beckworth couldn't *help* being dazzled. All right, she puts lots of ticks and stars and *Well Dones!* on his sections on railway engines and factories and coal mines, and she liked his town and country pages and all his maps in the British Empire bit, and she went a bit overboard on his Crimean War with an *EXCELLENT!* underlined. My postcards just got a tick or two, but that was obviously because she didn't want to deface the beauty of the page.

Miss Beckworth held Jamie's project up and showed it to the class and all the goodie-goodies went Oooh and Aaah and all the baddie-baddies went Yuck and Boring and Swot and Teacher's Pet. I would normally count myself the baddest baddie-baddie – and yet I found myself thumping old Jamie on the back and saying, 'Well done, Clever Clogs.'

He went very red when I said that. Maybe I thumped a bit too hard. Then he had to go up to Miss Beckworth and shake her hand and *she* said 'Well done' too. She said she'd like to give him a little prize. She gave him a £5 book token and a little painted Victorian soldier. Jamie was dead chuffed.

I couldn't help feeling a bit wistful then. I waited for Miss Beckworth to hand out the rest of the projects. I was sure mine would have red lines all through it and *SEE ME, CHARLOTTE!* in cross capitals. But you'll never ever guess what! Miss Beckworth paused theatrically.

'Jamie's brilliant project tells us almost all there is to know about Victorian times. But there's one other project here that tells us what it *feels* like to be a Victorian.' And she held out MY project!!! 'I'm so impressed with your diary of Lottie the Nursery Maid that I'd like to award you a prize too, Charlotte.'

'Great! Good for you, Charlie,' said Jamie.

Yep! Good for me! Miss Beckworth beckoned me out to the front of the class and I had to go through the hand-shaking ceremony too, which was OK – but I kept thinking, am *I* getting a prize like Jamie? And I did! A £5 book token, and a tiny reproduction china doll the size of my little finger.

189

'Oh, she's sweet! Thank you very much, Miss Beckworth,' I said.

'Do you know what they used to call that sort of doll? They were called Frozen Charlottes,' said Miss Beckworth, and she actually grinned at me.

I appreciated her little joke. I actually sort of appreciated *her* for once. She asked me to read out some of my diary entries for Lottie. So I did. Everyone got a bit shuffly and sighing to start with – but by the time I'd got to the bottom of the first page *they were riveted*! I read on and on and not a single person said Yuck, so there!

Lisa and Angela got a teensy little bit snotty afterwards. Lisa especially, because her dad had done all her Victorian project on his posh computer with special loopy writing and graphics and it hadn't even had a special mention.

'You're really getting to be a teacher's pet now, Charlie,' said Lisa. 'I don't know who's the swottiest now, you or your precious Jamie.'

'He's not mine. And he's not precious either, come to that,' I said, snorting.

'*We* saw you putting your arm round him when his project won,' said Angela, giggling away.

'Purlease!' I said. 'Don't be so pathetic, Ange.'

'You're the one that's pathetic, Charlie, getting all matey with Jamie Edwards. He's the nerdiest boy in the whole class.'

'So?' I said fiercely.

'So what do you *see* in him?' said Lisa.

'He can be quite good fun sometimes. OK, he

does look a bit weird—'

'You're telling me!' said Lisa.

'And he wears the grottiest clothes,' said Angela.

'Yes, right, he's a total Arnie-Anorak, but I don't care.'

'She's gone off her rocker,' said Lisa to Angela.

'Completely nuts,' said Angela to Lisa.

'Yeah, you're mad, Charlie. You could probably get any boy in our class keen on you – well, apart from Dave Wood – yet you choose *Jamie* for a boyfriend.'

'He's NOT my boyfriend. You two aren't half slow at catching on. He's a friend who happens to be a boy – OK a nerdy, grotty, swotty boy – but so what?' I shouted. A little too loudly. Jamie himself came out the boys' cloakroom and stared. Lisa and Angela doubled up laughing. I felt myself going red. Totally screamingly scarlet.

BRIGHT RED

'Better leave the two lovebirds together,' said Lisa, and she tugged Angela away.

They went giggle giggle giggle down the corridor.

'Idiots,' I muttered. I blew hard up my nostrils, fluttering my fringe. 'Phew, isn't it hot in here?' I paused. 'What are you staring at?'

'Did you just say I was nerdy and grotty and swotty?' Jamie asked.

'Oh,' I groaned. 'No.'

'I heard you,' said Jamie, looking wounded.

'Well, all right, yes. But it wasn't my description,' I said.

'So everyone thinks I'm nerdy and grotty and swotty,' said Jamie.

'No. Yes. Well, a few of the girls maybe. And the boys. Don't look all upset, Jamie, I'm trying to make things better.'

'I'd hate it if you were trying to make things worse then,' said Jamie.

'Look, you're not daft, you must have twigged that's what they think,' I said.

'You *are* making it worse,' said Jamie.

'But you don't really care, do you, Jamie?'

'Don't I?' said Jamie.

'Well, *I* don't care what anyone thinks of me,' I said.

'Yes, but that's because everyone likes you,' said Jamie.

'No they don't. Not even Lisa and Angela much, and they're supposed to be my best friends.'

'And . . . did you say *I* was your friend too?' said Jamie, looking a bit perkier.

I shrugged. 'Mmm,' I said.

'You mean it? We're really friends? Even though I'm a boy? And a nerdy grotty swotty one at that?' Jamie didn't seem at all upset now. I wondered if he'd been pretending before. I wouldn't put it past him.

'I generally can't stick boys,' I said. 'But you're OK.'

'So are you,' said Jamie.

We stood there looking at each other. For two ultra-chatty people we suddenly seemed lost for words. And then there were these s-t-u-p-i-d slurpy kissy-kissy sounds. Angela and Lisa had crept back towards us.

'Look at them!'

'Gazing into each other's eyes, dumb-struck!'

'Go on then, Jamie, kiss her.'

'They'll be snogging at the school disco next week!'

They collapsed with laughter.

'Take no notice,' said Jamie calmly. 'Let the lower mortals prattle.'

'You what?' said Lisa.

'He's talking in some foreign lingo now,' said Angela.

'See if you two can understand plain English then,' I said – and I used some very short sharp shocking words to indicate that I wanted them to go away.

'Who is using that disgusting language?' said a familiar voice.

A teacher came stalking down the corridor. The one with the all-hearing ears. You've guessed right.

She gave me a detention too, even though it wasn't really my fault at all that I'd been reduced to blunt language. But I still felt *quite* fond of her, even though she was always so snappily strict. So when our top year had our special disco party and Miss Beckworth organized it and asked us to bring some refreshments from home I went overboard.

I went round to Jamie's house and hunted through the Victorian books – and found a great big fat one with lots of recipes called *Mrs Beeton's Book of Household Management*. I flipped through it until I found the *perfect* cake.

It needed quite a lot of ingredients but that was no problem. (For reasons I will divulge later!)

It took ages to make the special cake. I had to make this special lemon jelly and then pour a little bit into a big tin and then stud it with glacé cherries like jewels, and then I did another layer of jelly and stood sponge fingers all the way round the tin and *then* I made a special eggy custard and poured that on and let it all set and THEN the next day I dunked the tin very quickly in hot water and then, holding my breath and praying, I gently tipped it out onto a pretty plate like a little kid turning out a sandcastle. You know what often happens with sandcastles? They crumble and break, right? But my special Victorian cake came out whole and perfect, easy-peasy, simple-pimple.

It was a bit of a mega-problem getting it to school, though. I had to carry it on a tray and hope it wouldn't rain. My arms were aching terribly by the time I got to school. I was a bit late too, because I'd had to walk so carefully to keep my cake intact.

'Charlotte Enright, you're late for school,' said Miss Beckworth.

'Only half a second, Miss Beckworth. And it's in a very very good cause,' I said, propping my heavy tray on a desk and peeling back the protective tinfoil I'd arched over it.

'And what's this very good cause, might I ask?' said Miss Beckworth.

'You!' I said, pulling the last of the foil off with a flourish. 'I've made you a cake, Miss Beckworth. Well, it's for all of us at the disco, but it's in your honour and you've got to have the first slice. It's a Victorian cake. And you'll never ever guess what it's called!'

Miss Beckworth looked at my wondrous masterpiece. She blinked her all-seeing eyes. They twinkled as she met my gaze.

'I *can* guess,' said Miss Beckworth. 'In your own ultra-irritating phrase, it's easy-peasy, simple-pimple! It's an absolutely magnificent Charlotte Russe.'

She really *is* all-knowing! We shared the cake-cutting ceremony when it was nosh-time. I got a bit worried my Charlotte cake would collapse, but it stood its ground splendidly. And it tasted great too, mega-yummy. It was all gone in a matter of minutes – just a lick of lemon jelly and a few sponge crumbs left on the plate.

I made sure all my special friends got a slice. Then the disco started up. It wasn't a *real* evening disco with a proper DJ and strobe lighting. It was just an afternoon Christmas party in the school hall for

195

Year Six, with the headmaster playing these mostly ropy old discs. Hardly the most sophisticated exciting event of the century – though you'd maybe think it was, judging by the fuss Lisa and Angela and some of the other girls made.

We were allowed to change into our own home clothes, you see. The boys didn't think it much of a big deal. They looked *worse* out of school uniform.

I didn't try too hard either. I was too busy creating my cake to fuss about my outfit. And I can't actually win when it comes to cool clothes way in the front line of fashion. My kit comes from the label-free zones of Oxfam, Jumble and Car Boot Sales, especially nowadays. Though this might change soon. (Second hint of changes in the Enright family fortunes!)

Lisa and Angela and lots of the other girls tried very hard indeed. Lisa looked particularly lovely.

But Angela was the big surprise. She usually wore ordinary old jeans and jumpers when we were hanging round after school. But now her mum had bought her this new party-time outfit down the market. Angela's got too tall for kids' clothes so this was really grown-up gear. And Angela looked ultra-adult in it too.

'Look at *Angela!*'

You couldn't help looking at her. Everyone did. It was as if she'd become an entirely new girl to match her new outfit. When she danced the boys all circled round. Even Dave Wood.

Jamie's jaw dropped when he saw Angela too, but he didn't try to dance with her. He didn't dance with anyone at first. I danced with lots of people. Then I went and stood near Jamie. I waited. It started to get on my nerves.

'Come on, Jamie. Let's dance,' I said commandingly.

'I don't think I'm very good at dancing,' said Jamie.

He was right about that. He just stood and twitched a little at first.

'Let yourself *go* a bit,' I said, jumping about.

Jamie let himself go a bit too much. His arms and legs shot out all over the place. I had to stay well back to stop myself getting clouted. But I suppose he was trying.

Lisa was standing near us. I prepared myself for some ultra-sarcastic comments. But Lisa's eyes were a little too bright, her smile showing too much teeth. She wasn't watching Jamie and me. She was watching Angela and Dave.

'Hey, Jamie. I want to dance with Lisa for a bit,' I said.

'Good! I need a rest,' Jamie puffed.

So I danced with Lisa for a bit. And then I danced with some of the other girls. And some other boys. So did Lisa. And at long last Dave Wood came slithering up to her, because he'd been elbowed away from Angela by the rest of the boys. I expected Lisa

197

to send Dave Wood off with a flea in his ear. I'd have added a swarm of stinging wasps and a buzz of killer bees. But would you believe it, Lisa just gave him this stupid smirk and danced with him devotedly. Lisa has got a very pretty head but it contains *no brain whatsoever*.

'Do you want to dance again, Charlie?' Jamie asked eagerly. 'I think I'm getting the hang of it now.'

He was a little optimistic. But we had fun all the same. The party ended at three and we were allowed to go home then.

Lisa and Dave Wood went off together, so she was happy.

Angela went off with half the boys in our class, so she was happy.

I decided to go back to Jamie's house because I was still a bit peckish in spite of my Charlotte Russe (the other refreshments weren't up to much) and I fancied one of his brother's toasted cheese sandwiches. We walked along Oxford Terrace together. I peered up at all the attic rooms right under the roofs and imagined Lottie looking out.

Jamie kept walking closer and closer to me, so that his schoolbag banged my shins several times. I turned to tell him off – and he kissed me on the cheek!

'What are you playing at?' I said furiously.

'I – I – well, you kept sticking your chin

up and looking up in the air so I thought you wanted me to kiss you,' Jamie stammered.

'Well, you got it seriously wrong, matie,' I said, giving him a shove. I scrubbed at the little wet patch on my cheek with the back of my hand. 'You do that again and I'll clock you one,' I said.

'Don't worry, I won't,' said Jamie. He sighed. 'I wish I could figure girls out. I especially wish I could figure *you* out, Charlie.'

'It's part of my deeply mysterious feminine charm,' I said, chuckling.

Jamie's brother came up trumps with another toasted sandwich and his mum asked if Jo and I could go round to their house on Boxing Day. They have a party every year. Jo got a bit worried when I told her and said she didn't think it sounded her cup of tea – well, glass of punch – but she's agreed to come with me because I've been astonishingly agreeable about *her* Christmas plans.

I shall give Jamie his Christmas present then. I've bought him a big fat paperback Victorian novel. *Jane Eyre* – by Charlotte Brontë, and inside the cover I've written: *This is a present by a Charlotte, from a Charlotte!*

I'm going to make Jamie's mum a special cake to eat at her party. I've got it all worked out. It's going to be a square cake, iced all over with a cake lid on top and marzipan ribbon, so it looks like a special gift box – for Boxing Day, get it?

I'm going to be so busy busy busy

199

making cakes in the Christmas holidays. I've got to make one for Grandma and Grandpa when Jo and I go over there on Christmas Eve – yuck! I had all sorts of good ideas but Jo talked it over with me and she thinks they'd like an ordinary conventional Christmas cake, white icing and HAPPY CHRISTMAS, boring boring boring – but I've said I'll do it.

I'm making one more cake – and this one's a special one.

Jo fixed a beautiful red breakfast in bed for us on Sunday (ruby grapefruit and raspberry Danish pastries and cranberry juice). When we'd eaten it all up we cuddled down in bed again and I started up one of our games and Jo tried to join in but I could tell she wasn't concentrating.

'Jo? What is it, eh?' I could feel her tense.

'Well . . . I want to talk to you about something,' she said.

I felt as if all the delicious red food inside me was being whisked in a blender. This was it. I knew what she was going to say. I wriggled away from her and lay stiffly in bed, waiting.

'It's about . . . Robin,' she said.

'And Mark,' I said, through clenched teeth.

'Well. Yes, I suppose so. Oh, Charlie. I don't know how ˌsay this.'

ˌay it for you,' I

ˌsy-peasy,

You

and Mark are going to get married and Robin's going to be my little brother and you'll be giving up all your jobs to look after him full-time and we'll have to sell our flat and go and live with them and I expect you want me to make you a flipping wedding cake as well, but if I have to come to your wedding I warn you, I won't throw confetti, I'll start throwing rocks at you,' and I turned over on my tummy and started to cry.

'What?' said Jo. '*What?*' And she started to laugh.

'It's not funny!' I sobbed. 'I want to stay here. With you. Just the two of us.'

'So do I,' said Jo. She shoved my tangled hair out of the way and said it straight into my ear. '*So do I!* That's what we're going to do. Now listen, Charlie! You've got it all wrong. Mark and I aren't getting married. He's still too fussed about his first marriage – and I don't think I ever *want* to get married. OK?'

'So you don't love him?'

'I don't know what I feel. I just want to let things develop. Slowly. In their own time. I hope I'll still see a lot of Mark and Robin – but I might not carry on working there. You know this Christmas job?'

You don't know about the Christmas job. Jo's stopped working at the Rosens'. The last big electrical goods shop in the town advertised for part-time staff to help them out over their busy Christmas trading time. Jo jumped in there and they took her on right away, working from nine to three. So we've got enough to keep up the mortgage payments – *and* a bit over. *That's* what I was hinting at earlier.

'You mean it's too tiring, working there and then going to look after Robin?' I said, leaning up on my elbows.

'The thing is, the shop manageress is going to have a baby. She wants to start her maternity leave in January – and even though I'm only temporary they're asking if I'm interested. It won't be for ever, of course, though she might decide she wants to stay at home with the baby – but it would still be great to get back to the work I like. But of course it would be full time, through till half past five.'

'I see. Well. You'll have to take it, Jo. I mean, it's great. But . . . what about Robin? He likes you a lot.'

'He likes you even more, Charlie. Mark hopes he'll be able to juggle his working hours and pick Robin up from school himself. Or maybe he'll have to find another child-minder. But in an absolute emergency I said you could always pick Robin up from school and look after him until Mark could come.'

'Mark wouldn't ever trust me with Robin!' I said.

'Yes he would. He knows that you're really very sensible and responsible,' said Jo.

'Me?' I said. 'OK. Tell Mark he can count on me. As long as he pays me!'

'Charlie!'

'So we can really stay here in our own flat, Jo?'

'You bet.'

'And we'll have our first Christmas here, just us two?'

'Ah. Well. That's the other thing I wanted to discuss.'

This time I did guess right.

'You want Robin and Mark to come round here for Christmas?'

'If that's all right with you, Charlie?'

I didn't want Mark to come at all. Still, it might be fun to have Robin bobbing about at Christmas.

So ... I decided I'd better come up with something pretty special for our Christmas cake. I baked a square fruit cake and then carved out part of the front and made up a brown butter icing and did this posh basket weave all over to make it look like ... a stable! With a big gold marzipan star and a fat pink marzipan angel perched on the roof.

(I'm going to get to eat the angel on Christmas Day – because I'm currently so angelic!) Then I made a marzipan Mary (Jo can eat her) and a marzipan Joseph (I suppose I *might* offer him to Mark) and a dear little marzipan baby Jesus clutching a white marzipan lamb (specially for Robin).

I piped a long message in front of all my Nativity figures.

PEACE ON EARTH.
GOOD WILL TO ALL MEN.

I never ever thought I'd be wishing Good Will to *any* man! I decided to add a bit.

AND GOOD WILL TO ALL WOMEN
AND BOYS AND ESPECIALLY GIRLS!

THE END